**PURE
SLUSH
BOOKS**

Feast!

Pure Slush Vol. 9

Pure Slush Books
4 Warburton Street
Magill SA 5072
Australia
Email: edpureslush@live.com.au
Website: http://pureslush.webs.com
Visit the Pure Slush Store: http://pureslush.webs.com/store.htm

Front cover photograph copyright © Cécile Graat
Back cover photograph copyright © Ramzi Hashisho

ISBN: 978-1-925101-62-1

Also available as an eBook:
Kindle ISBN: 978-1-925101-63-8 / ePub ISBN: 978-1-925101-66-9

A note on differences in punctuation and spelling

Pure Slush proudly features (both online and in print) writers from all over the English-speaking world. Some speak and write English as their first language, while for others, it's their second or third or even fourth language. Naturally, across all versions of English, there are differences in punctuation and spelling, and even in meaning. These differences are reflected in the stories *Pure Slush* publishes, and it accounts for any differences in punctuation, spelling and meaning found within these pages.

stories by

Paul Beckman

Claudia Bierschenk

Tom Fegan

Lyn Fowler

Desmond Fox

Gloria Garfunkel   Walter Giersbach

Kyle Hemmings   Gill Hoffs

Jonathan Levy

Cindy Matthews

AR Neal

Mandy Nicol   Matt Potter

Andrew Stancek

Susan Tepper

Michael Webb

Allan J. Wills

dedicated to

Consumpta Gorge

local tennis champion
and
dietitian with a secret

Adelaide, South Australia, Australia

The Conceit of This Book

Few things bring people together more often and more joyously than food.

Though of course, things go wrong. The food is burned, spoiled, undercooked, overcooked, too raw, too meagre, too dry, too moist, too hot, tepid, cold, overly-generous, not set and too runny, too solid, too crusty, too crunchy, old-fashioned, poisonous and worse: served at the wrong time or in a chipped or cracked dish!

It can also be fragrant, delicious and life-giving, and a great symbol of culture and status.

And is there a greater sign of affection than food lovingly prepared?

We all need it, even if intravenously or in pill form, and we all have relationships with it … even if we're not consuming any of it.

All stories in this book are set on the exact same day – Friday April 24th – and the book is structured so that each story is placed in correct international chronological order. The collection, in its page order, darts around the world as different characters experience food in their unique ways, often minutes apart, but all on the same day.

So it's a true feast day! Happy gorging!

Matt Potter, Pure Slush editor and publisher
April 2015

Adam Gets a Rude Awakening
by Mandy Nicol

Adam wakes to the whiz of the juicer. He groans, buries his head under the pillow, clamps it against his ears. The vzzzzz cuts straight through the orthopaedic natural latex foam rubber and pierces Adam's head somewhere behind his right eye. Adam slides out of bed.

He shuffles to the kitchen, yawning, and is greeted by his mother. She curls an arm around his head, kisses his forehead and hands him a glass of purple. Adam ponders the glass. Blueberry? He sips. Not blueberry. He smacks his lips at the earthy taste. His mother leans protectively against the sink so he has no chance of tipping it down the drain. He sits on a kitchen stool.

"Beetroot?" he asks.

"Yes! Do you like it? It's a glass full of goodness. Beetroot is another four-star superfood and, hang on." She picks up her health food book, opens it to a page tagged with a neon-pink post-it note. "... here, listen, *beetroot is a powerful blood cleanser and tonic, is good for the digestive system and liver, and has anticarcinogenic substances attributed to its red colouring.*" She smacks the book shut and smiles. It's a wide smile and Adam sees no trace of purple in or around his mother's mouth.

"Did you drink any of this goodness Mum?"

She puts her book on the bench. "No, but I would have if I'd had more beetroot."

"You can have half of mine," Adam offers.

His mother gazes out the kitchen window, says quietly, "Please drink it, Adam."

Adam takes a deep breath, closes his eyes and drinks the purple.

Now his mother can move from the sink.

She takes a plastic container out of the fridge and spoons fruit salad into two bowls. "Here, I'll have breakfast with you." She puts the bowls on the bench and sits next to him.

"Why is everything red?" Adam asks.

"It's a red fruit salad."

Adam swirls the salad around with his spoon, identifies strawberries, raspberries, grapes, watermelon, blood orange and pink grapefruit. An extension of the anti-cancer strategy, he thinks.

"Are you still planning to go to the beach today?"

Adam nods, manages to not roll his eyes to the ceiling.

"It's hardly beach weather, Adam, I don't understand why Jen can't come here, I could make a nice lunch for us all. It would be a lot more comfortable."

"Jen's already made a picnic lunch and sand can be very comfortable. And it's autumn, Mum, not the middle of winter. We're not going swimming so you have nothing to worry about."

Adam swallows the last piece of fruit and tips the bowl of juice into his open mouth. He smacks his lips together, enjoying the sweetness that has managed to revitalise his beetrooted taste buds. He takes his bowl to the sink, rinses it, returns to kiss his mother on the cheek. "Thanks for breakfast, Mum."

His mother grabs his arm. "You won't make it a long day, will you?"

"I'll be home by tea time." He wriggles his arm free before adding, "I'll even bring Jen in to say a quick hello."

"No, not a quick hello, bring her to tea! I'll try out a new recipe." She scurries across the kitchen to leaf through her health food book.

Every Meat This City Has to Offer
by Desmond Fox

I slip out of the hole into the uneasy orange city night. A slaughter of smells hangs heavy over the sun-beaten grass; fat pink meat, burnt flesh, petrol fumes, beer urine: barbeque season in the park.

The grilling section is a featureless scarred patch; approach with caution. Caution is a struggle after a day of cloistered sweltering inactivity, now broken by the thrill of so many jagged, contradictory scents.

I love summer in the city.

After picking my way around the skirt of bush, I nose for the first odour to capture me. Ohh, what's this? Where is it, where is it? Here a raw porkchop, last of the packet, still swathed in its broken crinkly wrapper, swimming in an acidic supermarket barbeque sauce. Tangy chomp chomp chomp. Such a delight: a delicious abstraction, meat devoid of its history. What a start.

Where next? A patch of lighter fluid. An empty crisp bag with a lick of salts and not too many spices. Shard of glass. Scattering of charcoal. A woollen garment with a sharp hint of perfume, a lower note of deodorant, and a trufflesque base note of staleness.

Next course: a sausage burnt on one side into stiffened rictus. Crunch. Satisfying resistance, and a contrast to the raw porkchop it squeezes from between my molars. Ironic how the food reaches the same exhausted state as the fuel used to cook it. The meat's last suggestions of flavour are overridden by the carbonised hide and its funereal associations. Overcooking never escapes a narrative of tragedy.

Here sat a circle of people, all leaving their own particular bum notes, a zodiac of psychedelic foulness. But here an especially flatulental impregnation, with a metallic menstrual bite. This species harangues the nostrils; rhymeless, chaotic; overfermented grains, rotten vegetables or any glomeration of foreign spices. Such confusion: too much for one species.

Enough with the park.

Departure
by Allan J. Wills

Every so often work takes me away from my family. It is honest work and it does no harm to anyone. Once in a while something of value to the greater good comes from it that seems to justify the effort of doing it. The only downside is going away from my family for four or five days, sometimes when everyone else is having a holiday long weekend. I have a little boy, just seventeen months, and he pines for me while I'm away.

On the morning of departure my little boy knows I'm going away, even when I pack my bag in the car the night before while he is asleep. I try to sneak out the door in the morning as on every other day when I work in the city office, but somehow he reads the clues in the body language between my wife and me.

"Dada, Dada!"

He clings to my legs, calling, and doesn't let go unless I pick him up and carry him. Eventually he allows my wife to carry him, and we hug him between us then wave goodbye to each other in the driveway.

I breakfast in the city at my desk: coffee and crepes from a café around the corner. There are always a few things to do in the office before I depart on these trips, emails that can't be ignored or deferred, confirmation of meetings with clients, so it's usually about ten in the morning when I get on the road and away. That is just fine as the freeway traffic has abated by then and I can set the cruise control and listen to classical music on FM.

Dog Shit
by Desmond Fox

*Two flies on an iron gate are watching a farmer herd his
cattle. One says to the other, "It is astounding what people
eat."*

The bitumen roadway is still sweating the day's heat into the
night air; an unusual sensation underfoot as I zigzag out of
the park. Along here one is assaulted by the effluvia of dogs.

However deep one's visceral contraction considering the
dietary habits of humans and their commensurate discharges,
the dog provokes a further retch. The house dog is a
terminally confused mongrel, always quarrelling with one
part of its nature, always searching for a middle rung in a
ladder of brutality. The sad, irreconcilable, hopeless hybrid,
equally dull and bombastic, is fully pronounced in the
loathsome qualities of its ordure, of which I shall say no
more.

Here is one of the park's wire mesh bins. And
conveniently outside of its skeletal grasp is a sweet little
delicacy; a diaper filled tight with baby urine. Such hope and
richness in one little package. Pastel pinks and blues. The
overspill of innocence.

The evolving technology of refuse storage has altered
the city's dietary landscape. The emphasis is on security,

which is a byproduct of fear. The ownership and responsibility regarding waste is resolved in these impervious, imperious, refusing bins that cover the exit of every supermarket and restaurant like defensive pillboxes.

Such nervousness over nothing, over what you'd rather be rid of, like a dog with full bowels holding on to project one last statement … for whom it may concern. Anyway, there is still plenty left to eat in this city, but not where it is collected.

There are these places where food is scattered in the night. The men who go to these centres become loud and disagreeable and throw away their meat having only chewed a few bites. I don't like the sauces too much: coarse, too vinegary. Like parenting birds, they half-digest the food and then spew it up on the pavements for us. Splat splat splat. That's not for me, but rodents see it as a delicacy.

Best to ignore people, don't even look at them, be prepared for a quick shimmy if they decide to throw something, can't expect people to change their instincts.

The city is sugar and fat, convenience and opportunity, and I wouldn't swap it. I'm not going to give you any of that Country Mouse and City Mouse bullshit. Danger is part of the bargain. I could live a lot longer in the country. But the diet? Chasing those skinny 'bio' mice? Give me the fast life. Sugars and fats.

Family Catch-up
by Matt Potter

"Grandma would *die* if she knew," my cousin Eve says, shaking her frizzy dyed-red hair. She rolls the dough in her hands into a ball, and pops the ball onto the oven tray. "She would curl her tiny middle-class toes up and have a heart attack. She's probably doing that just now, back in sleepy little old Adelaide, hey."

I smile – well, my mouth turns up a little at both edges – as Eve reaches into the bowl and scrapes the last of the dough into a ball with her fingers.

"Back in the Walkerville Methodist Cemetery," she continues. "Lying next to Grandpa."

"She's on top," I say. "Grandma's coffin's on top of Grandpa's."

Eve rolls the dough into a ball and pops it in the middle of the tray. There are seventeen dough balls on this tray, and sixteen on the other tray sitting on the draining board.

"This last one's for you, Carolyn," she says. "If you dare. If you can stop thinking like a bank manager's wife and live a little."

Eve is making Anzacs. Anzac biscuits have eight ingredients. I made them often enough with Grandma when I stayed at her house in the Hills when I was a kid, so I know.

You start with plain flour (sifted), rolled oats, caster sugar and desiccated coconut, combined in a bowl. Then place golden syrup (or treacle, if you don't know what golden syrup is) with butter in a saucepan, and melt them together. Then mix bicarb soda with a tablespoon of boiling water in a cup, and add to the melted butter mix. Watch it bubble up – kids really enjoy watching the bubbles reach the rim of the saucepan – then add the frothing mix to the dry ingredients. Combine all ingredients then roll into balls and place them on a greased or buttered oven tray, flattening slightly. Cook for about 12 minutes until golden.

I make Anzacs for every Anzac Day, April 25th, which is tomorrow.

It's an Australian tradition.

(Though you can make them any time, not just for Anzac Day. And you don't even have to be in Australia.)

Anzac Day is the day we remember all Australian and New Zealand servicemen and women who fought in wars. You can munch on the chewy goodness of an Anzac and think of all those who sacrificed their lives for us. People march in the streets and the really dedicated attend dawn services at their nearest war memorial, so it's a big, big deal.

And Anzac biscuits always have eight ingredients.

Except Eve's have a magic ninth ingredient.

Hash.

Eve is making hash Anzacs, which she doesn't think is sacrilegious.

Eve made the hash herself too, sifting the dried leaves and stems through a silkscreen then wrapping the powder in a freezer bag and then taping it up with sticky tape and then more and more and more sticky tape tighter and tighter and tighter so it's 100% waterproof and then boiling the package in boiling water for 7 minutes.

I guess that's why she lives near Nimbin, hippy capital of Australia.

My mobile *pings* but I don't bother to reach into my handbag (it's over on the coffee table, anyway) because I know it's another *When are you coming back?* message from Peter. *The kids are freaking out!*

And that's why I'm staying with my cousin because after 20 years of marriage, I don't know if I want to do it anymore.

"This is *not* sacrilegious," Eve says, as the oven door slaps shut on the two trays of hash Anzacs and she pushes her frizzy hair off her face with the back of her wrist. "It's *not*, Carolyn, it's just another way of celebrating our Australianness, that larrikin spirit, spitting in the eye of formality and all those pompous fuckers."

She smiles.

"They'll be just the thing at the poetry reading, too," she says, "all the poets will love them. Do they even have those in sleepy old Adelaide, hey?"

"Have what?" I ask.

"Poetry readings."

"I don't know," I say, "I don't even know if we have any poets."

Though with 1.3 million people, we probably do have a few poets. I just haven't met them.

You don't really get to meet poets when you're a bank manager's wife.

Now we're making a nut mix aka Nimbin Nuts. It's just a lot of nuts mixed together in a plastic bag – "Just a little sideline of mine," Eve says – with a bit of curry powder sprinkled over them then shaken and shaken and shaken 'til the curry coats them all. Brazil nuts and peanuts and pistachios – "Not macadamia nuts, though," says Eve, "they're fuckin' expensive, they're the rich man's nuts" – and cashews and pecans and walnuts.

Then more peanuts and more peanuts and more peanuts.

"They're not so expensive, peanuts are the poor man's nuts," Eve says, "that's why I'm happy to take them along for free. I always take Nimbin Nuts to the poetry readings, the Anzacs are just a special treat because it's Anzac Day tomorrow."

And that's when I remember, like a *ping* going off in my head. I remember how Eve has this thing for poets.

She's knotting the ends of a green and yellow sarong together, the knot flopping down her cleavage, her shoulders bare and brown above the bright new green and yellow material, and shining in the midday sun streaming through her open bedroom window. And I'm standing in the doorway. One arm folded across me, holding onto the other elbow.

"Did I ever tell you how I came to live in Nimbin?" Eve says. She fluffs her frizzy red hair out behind her shoulders and pulls the strapless sarong up under her arms, not five seconds after she's tied it up. She's gonna be in for a lot of sarong hitching the rest of the day, I can feel it.

"He was a poet, of course," she says, "Richard Stringfellow Longmuir de Cordé. He wrote the most exquisite rhyming couplets. Those couplets could make even the driest old maid wet. And I mean, *dripping*. Right there on the chair. A big old maid puddle in the middle of the rattan and velour."

Yes, in the family, I remember, Eve's nickname is *the poet-fucker*.

"And I know what you're thinking," Eve adds, "I know you're remembering my nickname is *the poet-fucker* in our wretched family. It's the only time they ever let themselves say *fuck*."

She slides the screen on her bedroom window across and reaching through the gap, picks a beautiful white flower from the bush growing outside in the garden. She pulls her frizzy hair back and sticks the flower behind her ear. Reaching up, she fluffs her hair again, then slides the window screen shut. She stands, looking me in the eye.

"And it's true, I am a poet-fucker, but I've only ever fucked the really talented ones, not the also-rans. I bet you don't have those in sleepy old Adelaide either, hey, any poet-fuckers? Because if you don't have poetry readings, how can the poets get to meet the poet-fuckers?"

I scratch my elbow and stare at the white flower bobbing behind her ear. I'm not quite getting her point.

I'm carrying the Anzacs and the Nimbin Nuts, following Eve as she walks out to her car. I'm wearing a green and yellow sarong too, but I've tied it around my neck, like a halter top, so I don't have to hitch the dress up under my arms every five seconds. I'm balancing the plate of Anzacs in my right hand and the dish of Nimbin Nuts in my left hand and I figured the balancing and the hitching wouldn't work.

("And you don't really have the shoulders for strapless," Eve said. "Funny how you're seven years younger but your shoulders are definitely much crépier than mine." Then she sniffed the sarong as she handed it to me. "That used to be my lucky sarong," she said. "There's a lot of juice in that fabric."

28

The sarong rolled out from my hands, exactly like the green and yellow Eve is wearing except older and faded and a bit frayed and holey around the edges. My skin is too pale and freckled for green and yellow, even faded and holey green and yellow, but I'm sort of at her mercy. I don't have any real money of my own and my aunt – Eve's mother – said she'd pay for my airfare here so I could get time away to think about not being a bank manager's wife any more.)

My bare feet scuff on the worn grass as we walk. I've become Eve's little project.

"One of the poets coming along today is really hot," she says. The door of her old Holden scrapes like a metal ratchet as she pulls it open. "He's talented but I reckon you'd suit him."

She slides in behind the steering wheel and reaching across the bench seat, the bangles on her arm fall past her elbow and jingle as she winds the window down then pulls the button up to unlock the passenger door. The car must be from the 50's or 60's and it's built like a tank, with big heavy doors, and through the window I can see red vinyl seats and a brown dashboard made of wood veneer and glass.

"I mean, he's not a brilliant enough poet for me but he'd probably be a good holiday fuck for you," Eve says through the open window. "Get in."

Eve turns the key and the engine coughs to life.

I'm standing by the passenger door with the plate of Anzacs in one hand and the dish of Nimbin Nuts in the other and I can't open the door. And the knotted ends of the faded green and yellow sarong are digging into the back of my neck.

12.50pm
Jan Juc, Victoria, Australia

Adam Gets Humble Pie
by Mandy Nicol

They lie on their backs beneath the cliff, heads almost touching, blond curls against brown spikes. One is tanned, one pale. T-shirts, jeans, bare feet. Their bodies form a vee, arrowing the rock wall.

"It's a long way up," says Jen.

Adam's eyes snap open. He squints at the cliff top.

"How high would it be?"

Adam has no idea but says, "A hundred metres, maybe more."

"As tall as the Eiffel Tower?"

"Doubt it."

"As tall as the Leaning Tower of Pisa?"

"I don't think that's very tall ... not as tall as it should be, anyway."

Jen laughs, sits up, crosses her long legs, shimmies around to face him. Adam turns on to his side to watch her. She has a long face and a long nose, matching her long limbs and long hair. Adam thinks it all fits together perfectly. His phone buzzes. He looks at the screen, taps it a couple of times and slides it back into his pocket. Jen tilts her head at him.

"Just my mum," he says.

"So why didn't you answer?" The silence stretches. Jen watches.

Adam finally says, "Whaaat? She only just saw me at breakfast. And she made me drink a bloody beetroot."

"Drink a beetroot?"

"Well, beetroot juice." Adam screws up his face. "It was revolting."

"Really? I've never tried it." Jen looks out to sea for a moment, then says, "Wouldn't she have added apples or something, to make it taste better?"

"I don't know about apples but I'm sure she jammed some of her favourites in there, like wheatgerm and cider vinegar and seaweed and, oh, maybe the turds of some obscure bat or something."

Adam laughs, so does Jen, but as soon as she stops she says, "You should have talked to her, she'll worry."

Adam sighs. "Yeah, I suppose."

Jen jumps to her feet, wriggles into her sandals, brushes the sand off her bum. Adam pulls out his phone and punches in a few letters, sends a short text to his mother.

Jen returns from the cliff with a picnic basket and cooler bag. "I hope you've still got an appetite," she says.

"As long as it's not beetroot salad."

"No, there's no beetroot and no salad. I've got egg and bacon pie, crusty rolls, and a surprise. Here, spread this out." She tosses a green tartan rug to him.

Jen butters the rolls and Adam slices pie. "This smells delicious," he says. "And it's a real pie! I thought you meant a quiche."

"No it's a pie pie."

"Where did you buy it?"

"I didn't buy it, I *made* it." Jen glares at him.

Adam doesn't notice because he's shoving forkfuls of pie into his mouth. "Wow," he says between mouthfuls, "I knew you were clever, but I didn't know you were *this* clever."

Jen grins, appeased. "Well it wasn't very hard," she admits. "Frozen pastry, eggs, bacon, oven. And that's about it!"

"You know what?" Adam smiles. "I don't remember the last time I had a meal without fruit or vegetables."

Jen laughs, reaches into the picnic basket, throws a mandarine at him, then another and another. Adam catches them, tries to juggle them, spills them on the rug. "So these are the surprise then, eh?"

"Oh no." Jen pulls a bottle of champagne and two plastic wine glasses out of the cooler bag. "This is the surprise. Happy three-month anniversary." She beams at him but Adam glances away, picks up the mandarines.

"Adam?"

"It's a lovely thought," he says.

"But?"

"I'm not supposed to drink."

Jen claps her hand against her mouth. "Oh God, I didn't think."

"It doesn't matter."

"Adam, I'm so sorry."

"It doesn't matter Jen, it's no big deal."

"Of course it's a big deal." Jen shakes her head, whispers, "How could I forget?"

"You know what?" Adam picks up her hand, squeezes it, says, "I *love* that you forget. I absolutely love it. Nobody else ever forgets."

6.00am
Cyclades Islands, Greece

Before Sunrise
by Lyn Fowler

It is before sunrise and we are dressed and up on deck. I taste the salty air. I am hungry and I have not even had a cup of tea yet. Our skipper is already at the wheel; the 40-foot yacht is ready. We are ready.

My husband, daughter, son-in-law and I met together with our skipper last night at the taverna and he showed us maps with the tide and weather forecasts. He had postponed our departure from the harbour because of the bad weather. The north-easterly wind across the Mediterranean, the Meltemi, had caused high winds and seas for three days. Our first instruction for this morning is to not eat or drink anything. Kostas was adamant. We were not to eat anything in the morning. Just get up on deck to be ready to leave with the tide. He repeated, "Nothing. Not biscuits. No, not tea or coffee. No, no, not water. Nothing!"

"Quickly, be ready!" Kostas now shouts over the rattle of the engine. We are motoring out of the harbour with no further delay and with nothing in our stomachs. Nothing to eat, Kostas had said, no water either. He was right of course and thankfully, our empty stomachs stay settled. The drawers in the galley slide open and closed as we cruise up and down with each crashing wave. It is exciting but I am not frightened. I look up at Kostas as he looks out on the sea and his boat. It is as though he knows each wave. With travel, you develop a sense of trust and the sharing of a meal reinforces that trust. I am glad that we shared our meal last night. The deal with the yacht charter means that you have to feed your skipper but for us it also means that we can get to know one another and we can together discuss the next few days. We were anxious to get going to enjoy our holiday but we are in the hands of a qualified seaman and he has to make any decision.

After half an hour of pounding waves, we round the point and anchor in a sheltered cove. It is calm here and the water inviting. Why not have a quick dip before breakfast. However, we are very hungry and the galley beckons. I climb down and find that all the fruit I had wrapped in tea towels is undamaged from the rough ride. The contents of the fridge are all still intact, even the eggs. The bottles of wine are secure. Our drinking water is sensibly stored in plastic containers.

"Anyone for poached eggs?" I call out from the galley.

"I thought we would be having scrambled eggs this morning," I hear my husband's voice from the deck.

"Well you can make the coffee, smarty."

Then I remember. Last night we dined at the harbour taverna and due to the bad weather, we were the only customers. We ate so much and went home back to our yacht with the leftovers. So this morning on deck into the bright sunlight I bring out the carefully wrapped and boxed food. There are delicious crispy tomato fritters that will be perfectly good cold, creamy fava bean dip and baked white eggplant, a sweeter cousin to the usual purple one, stuffed with tomato, onion, garlic and oregano. I will try to make my version of the fritters later. The ingredients are just finely diced tomato mixed with spring onions, parsley and mint and added to flour with baking powder. Spoonfuls of this batter are then deep-fried in olive oil. The favas are small dried yellow split peas boiled until a soft puree and then finished with lemon juice and olive oil and topped with capers. These vegetables do not require much water to grow and they must thrive in the less fertile soils of the islands. The result is concentrated taste. This is a feast of all breakfasts. Forget about bacon, eggs and toast. First, we must have coffee.

The coffee is brewing at last and the aroma is delicious. John pours the coffee for everyone into mugs.

Our skipper smiles at us. "What do you like to eat for breakfast, Kostas?" I ask.

"On the boat I only need orange juice and biscuits." He is very young with soft eyes and long eyelashes but he is the person you can trust to sail you around the world. He is content that he has safely skippered the yacht. The blustery wind is behind us now. Here in our cove the sun is shining, and the sea is calm. We are content sitting on the deck, enjoying our Greek island breakfast.

Poetry for Dummies
by Matt Potter

"The vagina wants what the vagina wants," Eve says. And then, smiling at the young guy with dreadlocks tied into a ponytail stretching halfway down his back, she points both her index fingers towards her lap and mouths, *It has a life of its own.*

Eve throws her head back and hoiks up a gut-busting laugh. The white flower behind her ear bobs and her red frizz flies out the full 360°. I lean back off my barstool as her laugh blasts me in the face. Dreadlock guy titters. Then both swig from their drinks, something green-looking that smells like crème de menthe and tastes like weedkiller. (I had a sip of Eve's, though only one.)

We're sitting in a triangle, on barstools in the Gloriana Room, waiting for the poetry to start. Except there's some time to kill and the poetry is being written while we wait.

I look about the room. There's not a lot of gloriana about it, beige walls and odd tables and chairs and barstools, poets scribbling away on ripped up paper with nibbled-on pens. The bar looks like an old bamboo reception desk from a tropical hotel. And so does the barman behind it, face and neck shiny with sweat and eyelids hanging down over his eyeballs.

Eve pushes the plate towards dreadlock guy. "Have an Anzac."

"Don't mind if I do," he says, picking one off the plate. He bites into it and the bite snaps off in his mouth. "Yeah, I'm taking a break from iambic pentameters," dreadlock guy says, nodding, chewing, grinning. "Like a holiday but just for the weekend."

"Carolyn here's from Adelaide, just sort of for the weekend too," Eve tells dreadlock guy. "She's just left her husband who's a bank manager. She's staying with me trying to get back in touch with Life, hey."

"Mmm, Adelaide," dreadlock guy says, popping a stray crumb in his mouth with a finger.

His face is tanned and his blue eyes twinkle when he breaks into a smile. He must be in his late twenties but it's hard to tell beneath the tan. His skin is leathery and dusky and dry. Maybe he's so chilled out he doesn't need to shower.

Dreadlock guy swallows and says, "Mmm, great Anzac."

He puts the hash Anzac down on the bar and picks up his glass again.

"It's our grandmother's recipe," I say.

I sip my bush lemonade, served in a bamboo flask with a paper straw. (Dunno what bush lemons are, but bush lemonade tastes just like normal sugary and sour homemade lemonade to me.)

"Well, it's Grandma's recipe without the hash," I add.

"What is it about you people from Adelaide, hey?" Eve says, but she turns to dreadlock guy and shrugs her bare shoulders, tossing her hair again. "It's like you've all had the adventure bred out of you."

I smile – well, my mouth turns up a little at both edges. "How old were you when you left Adelaide, Eve?" I ask.

Dreadlock guy tilts his glass in my direction. "Don't knock Adelaide," he says. "I've had some great times in *Radelaide*." And smiling at me, he sips his drink again. And then, putting his glass back down on the bar he says, looking at me, "That's a beautiful sarong you're wearing."

I peer down at my cleavage, which is nowhere to be seen, entirely hidden by the faded green and yellow fabric. The knotted ends of the sarong digging into the back of my neck are giving me a neck ache.

"Yeah, it's mine," Eve says. "It used to be my lucky sarong but I had to trade it in for this one." And arching her back, she sticks her breasts out and sticks her bottom out and somehow still manages to stay upright on the barstool. "Exactly the same fabric, just brand *spanking* new."

Eve's bangles jingle on her arms as she claps her hands together right beside my ear. (I almost jump off my stool!) A man in a heavy brown t-shirt and black shorts stands on the podium set up in the back corner of the Gloriana Room. He bends towards the microphone but the first sound out of his mouth is silenced by the *CCCRRRRRRR!!!!* of screeching grating metallic feedback.

I clap my hands on my ears, as brown t-shirt guy steps back a little and says, feedback-free, "Whoa." And then, deep and throaty, he adds, "I'm the Pyjama Poet. But most people call me Rocket."

"Oh yeah, Rocket," Eve says, not really to anyone.

The crowd – about twenty, hard to tell just how old they are because they all look like dreadlock guy, dusty and brown and leathery – clap their hands above their heads. Eve cups her hands and *Whoop Whoop*s at the ceiling and her bangles jingle again. Dreadlock guy grins and nods some more as he swallows the last of his third hash Anzac.

"This is a poem I wrote called *The Orgasm Big Enough for Two*," the Pyjama Poet / Rocket says, then he grunts into the microphone.

I reach into the bowl of Nimbin Nuts. Biting into a brazil nut, all I can really taste is the curry powder coating my tongue.

"You can call me Nesbitt," dreadlock guy says. His eyes are red and his nose is red and his lips are green (from that weedkiller drink). He sticks his hand out and I shake it. It's like a wet fish in my palm.

"Okay," I say, though I'm not sure if that's his name or he's just making it up. Or maybe he meant his hand is called Nesbitt. Maybe he has a talking hand and it's part of his poetry act.

"This is a poem I wrote called *The Orgasm That Saved the World*," the Pyjama Poet / Rocket says, still standing on the podium. Then he grunts into the microphone again.

The crowd clap their hands above their heads again and Eve cups her hands and *Whoop Whoops* at the ceiling again. Her damn bangles jingle. Then she turns to me and through the bright green and yellow fabric of her sarong, rubs her fingertips against her nipples. "I think I'm going to fuck him," she says.

I look at her. I don't know what she wants me to say.

"I bet no one ever does that in Adelaide, hey?" Eve asks.

"Does what?" I ask, though I don't know why, because Eve is looking at Nesbitt now and Nesbitt is looking across the crowd at the Pyjama Poet.

I reach into the bowl of Nimbin Nuts. There are only peanuts left – I've eaten all the other nuts – so I chew on some peanuts and that's when I see Nesbitt has his hand down his shorts. And his other hand is stuffing another hash Anzac in his mouth.

"Yeah," Eve says, looking from Nesbitt to me and then back to Nesbitt and then at the poet on the podium and then back at Nesbitt. "I'm definitely going to fuck him." And then she looks at the poet again and then out of the corner of her eye, she glances at Nesbitt. "Definitely, right after his last poem."

I ferret in the bowl of Nimbin Nuts. There's one brazil nut that looks a bit dodgy – green and furry, even through the curry coating – so I grab a handful but push the bad nut aside. I toss the rest into my mouth.

Nesbitt stuffs another hash Anzac into his mouth, whole. Luckily, his mouth is wide enough to take it. And he still has his other hand tucked inside his shorts. Which looks like it's drumming *something* but I can't really tell because I'm not a drummer.

Eve steps around me and grabs Nesbitt by the shoulders. Her fingers push down, down, deep into his muscles.

"Ow!" Nesbitt says, but he just sits there anyway, hand in his shorts, as Eve stands behind him, kneading his body, bangles jarring.

"I really need to fuck that poet," Eve says, her eyes dark as she works her thumbs into Nesbitt's neck. "But I need to work off this tension too."

I grab at the Nimbin Nuts but there's nothing to grab except the dodgy brazil nut. I peer into my bamboo flask but yeah, I drained it of bush lemonade a while ago.

The Pyjama Poet steps away from the microphone, but a beat later he's back up there and speaking again.

"This poem is called *The Big O*," he says. "But it doesn't stand for *Orgasm* ... it stands for ... *Opening*."

Eve stops kneading Nesbitt's shoulders to cup her hands and *Whoop Whoop*s at the ceiling again again and the crowd clap their hands above their heads again again.

"Oh God," Eve groans, "he's making me so wet." She shakes her head loose, and the white flower falls from behind her ear, onto Nesbitt's shoulder and then drops to the floor.

Nesbitt giggles. "The Pyjama Poet has a big cock," Nesbitt says, looking down at the white flower, beside my foot on the floor. "I saw it once, in the toilets."

"Yeah," Eve says, as her fingers knead. "*Rocket.*"

Nesbitt titters. His green lips are wet with saliva and he grins, his tongue covered in hash Anzac crumbs. He swallows. "That's not why they call him *Rocket.*" He slips forward off his barstool. "I need a piss."

Eve reaches into the Nimbin Nuts on the bar and grabs the only nut left, the dodgy brazil nut. She screws her face up at the taste but chews and swallows anyway.

"Nabisco's yours, if you want him," she says. She stands, pelvis thrust forward, hands on her hips. Together we watch Nesbitt weave his way through the crowd, towards the toilets.

"He likes a bit of Adelaide," she adds.

"His name is Nesbitt, I think."

"Well, he's yours," she says. "Jeez, too stoned to get a hard-on while I'm massaging his shoulders and talking about getting wet."

I nod. I don't know why though. Maybe it's the Nimbin Nuts making me do it.

Eve cups her breasts with her hands and she shakes her head loose again, red frizz flying as those bangles screech.

She does this so often it's getting kind of annoying. Maybe it's a tic.

"I'm gonna get me some poet," she says, wiping the curry powder from her lips on the back of her hand. "Don't wait up. You could be back in Adelaide by the time I get back." And she steps away from the bar and into the crowd.

6.00am
Berlin, Germany

6.00am Feed
by Claudia Bierschenk

He's made his body from mine. He's got perfect little fingers, toes, eyelashes, and earlobes. And in the two months that he's been in this world, he hasn't eaten anything that didn't come from within me. I am his only source of food.

12.10pm
Donnybrook, Western Australia, Australia

Café Tiffany's
by Allan J. Wills

Two and a quarter hours down the track it's lunch time. Each trip I stop in the same small town for lunch. I've tried all three of the town's cafés and the bakery during my many trips away. The bakery has good pastries, reasonable rolls and sandwiches but bad coffee. One café has good burgers, an excellent chicken Caesar salad and average coffee. Another café has average coffee but bland food. Now I lunch at Café Tiffany's.

I don't stop especially for the food, which includes a tasty vegetarian selection and comes in generous portions, or the coffee, which is good too but sometimes tends to be a degree too milky. For some reason the owner has a thing about Audrey Hepburn. There are various photos of Audrey on the walls, all showing her beauty, gamine and chic and at the height of her stardom. There is even a biography of her among the newspapers and magazines on the buffet, bound in coffee table format with many photos from across her life. The blackboard menu boasts all-day breakfasts. Maybe the owner of the café is named Tiffany and is playing on *Breakfast at Tiffany's*. It's a hypothesis. The facts are likely to be much simpler. I guess I could ask the cashier sometime, but that doesn't matter so much to me. I stop there to see one particular photo of Audrey. Having a pleasant lunch too is a convenient extra.

I order the Quiche Lorraine and a mug of coffee and take a seat opposite the photo while waiting for the food to arrive. In the black and white portrait Audrey is in her mid-twenties and standing under what appears to be the foliage of an olive tree. Her arms are raised and frame her face. The photographer, Philippe Halsman, has captured the slightest trace of pensive vulnerability along with her beauty. Perhaps she has just discovered that Halsman has fallen in love with her. I have seen this expression somewhere else: on my wife, in the earliest days of my love for her.

Audrey is long deceased. She's timeless now, living only on film as Holly Golightly on the crazy quest of looking for her cat in the rain with Paul Varjak.

When I first saw my wife in Audrey's expression I felt a pang in my heart so intense and sharp. Now the fleeting expression captured in the photograph affects me less. It serves to remind me of the bond between my wife and me. Two and a quarter hours down the road from home I think of that and I think of her looking after our little boy.

7.00am
Bratislava, Slovakia

Tripe Soup
by Andrew Stancek

David yawns. Another night when he's slept no more than three hours, and the throb behind his eye is like a dentist's drill. The rooster which used to wake him at daybreak now crows throughout the night and screeches in his ear.

David runs to catch the streetcar, trips, the loose shoe catapults into the gutter but he grabs the rail and pulls himself onto the landing as the clanging streetcar gathers speed. He hates those brown slip-ons with the silly tassels and glares at the scuffed right shoe, lopsided in the downpour. He crashes onto the orange plastic seat. At work he has a pair of dress shoes and in the meantime, no one he knows will see him, barefoot. His toe throbs but it isn't bleeding. His stomach grumbles. If he'd missed the streetcar he would have been half an hour late but now he'll be able to stop in at the cafeteria on Sturova, grab a Turkish coffee.

A man, maybe two years older than David, with his arm around a six-year old, moves his son's head to stifle the giggles at David's bare foot. The father shrugs apologetically, and David wiggles his toes for the boy's benefit, who sprays snot in laughter. The rain pounds against the window and on a fence a sparrow shivers.

Ever since Taia left he cannot eat. Yesterday he threw away the half-eaten *wurst* that had briefly seemed appetizing, then walked into a pastry shop for chestnut purée

46

with whipped cream. But at the counter the thought of sugar revolted him and he scurried out clutching his stomach. He sees Taia's scarf, her coat, her skirt twenty times a day, on every Bratislava street, but when he runs up, grabs a sleeve, another woman snarls. At night he drinks liters of sparkling mineral water, recites Halas and Seifert and pisses. His boss told him he looks like shit and stinks. David walks around the flat, sniffing for Taia remnants. In the bathroom, next to the nail file, he finds a perfume bottle with a few drops at the bottom, and he undoes the stopper and inhales. He screams from the diaphragm, just like his music teacher taught, years ago.

If he loses his job he'll have to join the homeless on the other bank of the Danube, by the bridge. He hates the pointlessness of checking endless invoices, but knows there's no way in hell he can make it on the streets. He remembers being told that what kills the jumpers is not the drowning in the Danube but breaking their neck from the impact. He loves answers to odd questions but isn't sure who to ask. Probably a broken neck is faster, more merciful. His friend Karol's mom slit her wrists in the bathtub and Karol says that years later, he still feels blood on his skin after a bath. David shudders. And hanging, eyes bulging, tongue sticking out, pants full of shit – too grotesque.

Taia said he was self-obsessed. David knows he's the very milk of kindness. He offers his seat to seniors on the bus, helps a blind man across the street, joins the rescue team for a lost child. What she meant is that he doesn't pay her enough attention. She needs to be the center, always. And David worships her but he is lost in his thoughts, and forgets what he promised and where he said he'd be. He looks up, notices a kite, wonders how it's possible to catch the gusts and fly forever and suddenly he's stood Taia up again. He doesn't blame her for leaving, but doesn't know how to change.

He knows the sharp pain in his chest is not a heart attack. It's a void – she ripped his heart out.

The streetcar makes a right by the Carlton Hotel and stops. David hops off. He takes a few limping steps, decides he's too ridiculous, kicks off his left shoe in a huge arc, watches it plop into a puddle. Barefoot is more sensible, even on cobblestones in the center of town. He drags his feet through puddles, the water chilling his toes. Forget coffee and a sweet, he decides, he'll have tripe soup for breakfast, with an extra piece of rye bread, and a pickle, straight out of the barrel. They probably don't have the schnitzels ready yet, barely eight in the morning. He pushes the door of the cafeteria open, is slammed with the sharp smells of frying onions, spilled beer, *debreciner* sausage. He shuffles to the end of the line-up of yawning workmen in grimy overalls. The woman in the green blouse runs up to him, grabs his cheeks between her meaty hands and kisses him hungrily. David is stunned. She breaks the kiss, slaps him, rattling his head. "Swine," she spits. She runs out the door and David's eyes follow the jiggling behind.

"I'll also need a shot of slivovica," he decides.

Talisman
by Allan J. Wills

It's half an hour to where I'm going. The client is expecting me at 3:00 pm. He likes to discuss business over tea and homemade cakes, showing off his wife's baking prowess. I'll arrive early at this rate so first I have one more stop.

In another town along the highway is a secondhand and antique shop. I call by there every couple of trips to check out new stock. I sometimes find an inexpensive gift for my wife. A man having an affair with another woman often attempts to reconcile his guilt by showering his wife with gifts. There is no guilt in my acquaintance with Audrey Hepburn's portrait, yet I'm not sure why I buy these gifts. When I give them to my wife she scolds me for wasting money on useless junk. Gifts aren't her love language.

Once, I found a Synyer and Beddoes hallmarked silver match case engraved with my initials. What are the odds of finding something like that with your own initials? This time I see a pewter thimble with lucky horseshoe motif tucked away in the corner of a display cabinet.

"May I look at the pewter thimble? The one there in the corner at the back."

"It came in an old sewing box amongst everyday things. I have better ones too, silver or porcelain."

Close up on my finger I see its rustic, home-crafted optimism, much like the ring from the crackerjack box presented to Holly Golightly. The sticker on the back says ten dollars.

"I'll take it for ten dollars!"

"I mustn't have put a high enough price on it," the proprietor laughs.

We talk about some other things in her stock before I bid my farewell. Now I must get to where I'm going, do my work and return home. A thimbleful of luck will see me safe.

Emergency Dash
by Matt Potter

The driver's door of the old Holden slams with a heavy *shtoock* and green and yellow material and frizzy dyed-red hair flash in front of the windscreen. Eve's bare feet slap on the concrete footpath as her bangles jingle and my mobile *pings* again from inside the glove box then there's a long moan from the back seat. In the distance, a toilet door bangs shut, and then the body in the back seat groans and rolls and moans some more and the car keys tinkle from the lock behind the steering wheel.

So there's a lot of action. And not a lot of it good.

"Stop it, stoooooppp it," Nesbitt moans from the back seat. "It's a human rights abuse ..."

I don't want to go there, so I sit still in the front passenger seat.

I do this for five minutes – so a lifetime – but then think, so what do I do now? I could open the car door and slip onto the grass by the roadside and slowly walk up the concrete path, past the swing and the seesaw and the slippery dip and the sandpit and that whirly thing and all the other empty play equipment and stand at the door to the toilet block and ask, *Are you okay, Eve?*

I could do that.

And then have her say, *Bet no one ever gets diarrhoea in sleepy old Adelaide, hey Carolyn? Because everyone's arsehole is wound up too tight, hey.*

I flip open the glove box and pull out my mobile. There's another message from Peter. *The game is up Carolyn,* the message says. *Justin's on the roof and Natasha's choking on popcorn! We need you back home.*

I stow the mobile back in the glove box and slap the door shut.

"Ow!" Nesbitt says from the back seat. "Stop the ship, it's sinking!"

I could turn around and make cooing noises at Nesbitt over the back of the bench seat.

I turn around and look over the back of the bench seat. Saliva is frothing at the corners of Nesbitt's mouth and his hands are swatting at his crotch.

"Stop the vaginas," he whispers, his hands flapping and his head thrashing and his dreadlocks whipping against the hash Anzac plate on one side on the seat and the bowl empty of Nimbin Nuts on the other. "Pleeeasse, make the vaginas stop."

I turn back to face the front windscreen, then reach behind my head and pull away the halterneck knot still digging into my neck.

Eve's hand was resting on the Pyjama Poet's arm when she suddenly clutched her stomach with her other hand and bolted out of the Gloriana Room. I was watching them. I was talking to Nesbitt (well, really, he was dribbling because he'd polished off all the hash Anzacs by then) and watching Eve trying to seduce the Pyjama Poet, when she made her emergency dash.

I left Nesbitt dribbling on his stool by the bar. Knocking on the cubicle door, I said, "Are you okay, Eve?"

She groaned and then I heard a lot of splashing echo inside the toilet bowl and then Eve said, "Has he gone?"

She probably means the Pyjama Poet, I thought.

"Who?" I asked.

"The Pyjama Poet," she said. "Rocket."

"Yes, I think so," I said, "though I'm not 100% sure."

Although, actually, I was about 99% sure he was still there, but that would be telling.

"Yeah, he is gone. He left with that tall blonde woman. The one he kept looking over at when you were talking to him."

Eve errggghed. Her voice sounded like it was bouncing off the floor tiles, like she was bent over at right angles, her head between her knees. "If Rocket has gone then I want Nabisco for myself," she said. "If you're feeling lonely I've got an old dildo you can borrow. I don't want you to feel left out."

So her vagina still meant business.

I pulled open the door to the Gloriana Room and stood in the doorway. Poetic murmurs floated through. The door creaked as I opened it wider, and giggles filtered through to join the poetic murmurs.

"That's okay," I said. "Nesbitt said he knows from personal experience that Rocket has an enormous penis, and there's never a dry eye in the house when he's around."

I rap my knuckles on the cubicle door. "Are you okay, Eve?" I ask. My voice sounds like a cartoon character because I'm breathing through my mouth and speaking through my nose.

The toilet block smells like ... well, a filthy, disgusting toilet block besides a public playground. Diarrhoea and stale filth and old sweat and those sugary sweet yellow blocks they leave in urinals that look like boiled sweets.

"I will be," she groans, like her body is at right angles again. Followed by more sounds of fluid gushing into the toilet bowl. "You need to go back to the car to make sure Nabisco doesn't escape."

I look down at the frayed hem of the faded green and yellow sarong.

"Nesbitt," I say. "His name is Nesbitt. And I don't think Nesbitt likes women," I add. "I might be from sleepy old Adelaide but that's one thing we do have, men who appreciate big penises."

"I have a very powerful vagina," Eve says. "It doesn't take no for an answer."

There's another groan from Eve, followed by yet more slop flowing into the toilet bowl.

"But is there anything left of it in there?" I ask.

"Of course there is!" she snaps. "Just make sure Nabisco doesn't escape!"

Back at the car, I see the hash Anzac plate and the Nimbin Nuts bowl on the back seat, but no Nesbitt.

My mobile *pings* again so I reach in through the open passenger window, snap open the glove box and take out my mobile. Just as I straighten up and begin pressing buttons to check another message, I see something over the car roof. Nesbitt is standing on the other side of the road, staring at a bush covered with bright pink hibiscus flowers. They're all over it, and some are scattered on the grass beside it too.

"Nesbitt!" I call out.

He turns and grins. He has pink all over his teeth and lips. "Mmmm," he says, and stuffs another flower in his mouth.

Feet slap up the concrete footpath. "Get in the car!" Eve yells out. "The day isn't over yet and my vagina's growling!"

But then her face screws up and a big watery fart echoes across the playground. Dyed-red hair spins around and knees clutched together, bangles a-jangling, Eve hobbles back towards the toilet block.

A car speeds past, roof open and folded down. Rocket, the Pyjama Man sits in the front passenger seat beside the tall blonde woman he kept looking over at when Eve was talking to him. They smile as they sail past. They wave as their hair flies behind them. They cheer as they toot their horn.

Across the road, Nesbitt falls to his knees. Lying beside the hibiscus bush, he has his hand tucked inside his shorts again, a pink flower gripped in his teeth.

I smile – well, my mouth turns up a little at both edges – and start punching buttons on my mobile to call home.

Homegoing Day – Morning
by AR Neal

"Taste this," Nancy ordered as she shoved a spoonful of macaroni salad in Jamal's mouth. "Is it enough tuna? You know how Bertram and them like it with a lot of tuna." She put her other hand on her hip. "Lord knows they never lift a finger to buy a single can but they sure want to tell you how to make it."

Jamal licked mayonnaise from the corners of his mouth. He had come for the rest of his glass of sweet tea from dinner and instead found himself wrangled by his mom in a kitchen full of burbling pots and pans.

"You know, Daddy loved daffodils. I bet he'd be disappointed to see how the cold did them this year," Nancy said as she turned back to the little window over the sink and squinted into the dark. It was only 4.00am but her potato salad needed just a few more ingredients. She had so much to do.

Jamal scratched his neck. "Ma, why are you cooking? Auntie Stella said —"

"Boy, you know Stella can't cook. Besides, everybody's gonna be looking for my potato salad." She whipped the big spoon around the silver bowl until it sang.

Jamal watched, hypnotized by the rhythm of her wrist. "So?"

"So what?"

She stopped stirring and looked at him over the tops of her glasses. "The macaroni salad?"

"Oh! Yeah, it's great. But what is all this?" Jamal asked as he waved a hand across the kitchen. "You should be resting."

"What in the world do I have to rest for? Daddy would be cross if I didn't feed these people right, today of all days."

Jamal tiptoed to the refrigerator and opened the door. He had put his glass at the back of the first shelf, which was now filled with rainbow gelatin molds. He checked behind each one and sighed; he surveyed the kitchen again and spied his now-empty glass as it sat on a pile of dirty dishes.

"Boy, shut that ice box before you let all the cold air out."

Jamal walked to the sink, rinsed the glass, and filled it with tap water. "Ice boxes went the way of the dinosaur, Ma. What you have there is an energy-efficient piece of 21st century technology." He paused to savor a swallow of water and grimaced. He had become accustomed to his filtered city water; distance and time had changed many of the old country homestead's flavors in the five years since he had left home. Jamal Washington was on his way up the ladder of success and the timing of this particular family issue could not have been worse. He thought there was nothing left for him in the neighborhood and shook the thought away quickly; his family was there and that certainly was more than nothing.

He watched his mother as she dolloped mayonnaise and mustard on top of the perfectly-cubed potatoes in her shiny bowl. "Anyway, like I said, you need to rest. Besides, nobody's gonna want any kind of salad for breakfast. I think Uncle Bud is getting something catered in."

Nancy stirred the seasonings into the potato salad. "You know you want some of this good cookin'," she teased. "Go

57

look in the stove."

Jamal turned on the oven light, cursed under his breath when it did not come on, and gently cracked the door to peer inside. "Ma, one of the first things I'll do when I get back is buy you a stove. This thing is so old, Methuselah's momma probably baked the first loaf of bread in it."

Nancy stopped stirring and frowned. "Boy, watch your language. Besides, nobody asked you to buy me a stove. Daddy had that put in here when he bought me this house. Now look in there like I said," she admonished.

Nancy's egg and bacon casseroles were heavenly and Jamal felt the water rise in his mouth. He shut the oven. "Uncle Bud's gonna be mad. There's enough casserole for twenty people in there, and I think he already paid."

"You wanna clean this for me?" She had left a big dollop of salad on her stirring spoon and Jamal chewed his bottom lip as he took it. "Do I look like I care if Bud paid for anything? Nobody asked me what I wanted." Nancy fussed as she ripped a gossamer piece of plastic wrap from the tattered box on the counter and covered the bowl of potato salad. "Don't nobody want that old dried up diner food he bought."

Jamal bucked his eyes at her and she shrugged.

"That's what Bud always gets for family gatherings. Calls himself catering. That's not catering," she mumbled, as she stacked the trays with olives, cheese, and salami to make room in the already-packed refrigerator and slid the potato salad bowl between savory macaroni salad and glistening Ambrosia.

Jamal looked at the spoon. No one made potato salad like his mother. She had shared a few of her precious recipes with him before he had moved away but her versions always came out better. He smiled at her and asked, "Why must you be so contrary, Ma?"

Nancy turned down the flame beneath her pressure

58

cooker and stepped across to the sink to pour water off the hardboiled eggs. As she tilted the steaming pot she said, "I need to keep busy."

"It's four in the morning, Ma. Ain't that much busy in the world."

"You didn't say that when Daddy caught you sneaking back in the house that time you and Jimmy called yourselves clubbing all night. Y'all got real busy when he was ready to put you on punishment." Nancy lifted the edge of her apron and pretended to tap dance. "I don't think I've ever seen the two of you think up lies so quick."

Jamal laughed at his mother and the memory. He had been eighteen and it felt like a lifetime ago when his dad had threatened to take his head off his shoulders if he ever disrespected the house by staying out past midnight ever again. He wondered who would chastise him now that his dad was dead.

"Jamal?" Nancy looked at him again over the tops of her glasses. "You all right?"

"I'm good, Ma," he answered as casually as he could and fingered a foil-covered mound on the corner of the table. "Might there be cornbread rolls under here?"

Nancy beamed. "Of course." Jamal peeled back a corner and carefully removed two rolls; Nancy always stacked them in a spiral and the ones he chose would not ruin the pattern. "Don't you mess up my pattern, boy," she chided out of habit.

"Tsk! You know I got it." Jamal sucked his teeth and handed her a roll. "I know you got some warm butter. Let's do this." He found an empty bar stool; the rest were covered with trays of crackers and bowls filled with freshly-washed fruit.

Mother and son stood next to each other, savoring the grainy rolls.

Nancy wiped crumb-covered fingertips on her apron

with a sigh. "I sure miss Daddy."

"I know, Ma," Jamal replied. He had no idea since this was his first experience with death but placing an arm around her shoulder, he tried to hug the sadness from his mother's face. "Say, why don't you go put your feet up? I'll wash dishes right quick."

"Thank you, son," her voice trembled. She turned away to wipe a tear and Jamal looked out the window. "Jamal? You heard from Jimmy? Do you think he'll be here?"

He frowned. "I don't know, Ma. You know I went looking for him when I first got here. I gave a message to one of his *associates*," he spat the word. "He knows, Ma. That's all I can tell you."

"You're a good boy, Jamal," Nancy said gently. She peered through the window into the yard. "At least the azaleas did well. You know Daddy loved azaleas."

Jamal sank his hands into the sudsy water. "I know, Ma," he offered with a smile, "I know."

6.40pm
Geelong, Victoria, Australia

Adam Gets a Raw Deal
by Mandy Nicol

"Are you sure we can't give you a hand, Mum?" asks Adam.

Adam's mother shakes the colander of pasta over the sink. "No, it's pretty much all done." She tips the pasta shells into a large bowl then looks across at Adam and Jen sitting at the dining table. "There's nothing to it. The trick is to keep the pasta *and* the broccoli *al dente.*"

"Which translates to *raw*," Adam whispers to Jen.

Adam's mother raises her eyebrows at him then nods to the far end of the kitchen-dining-lounge room. "Jen, have you seen the photos of Adam when he was young? He was such a sweet little boy."

Jen crosses the room and sidles along the wall as if she's at an art gallery. Which she sort of is.

Adam's mother tips a pan of bright green broccoli onto the pasta, adds a pat of butter and a cup of grated parmesan.

Family photos in rustic timber frames are arranged randomly but artistically on the wall. Most feature Adam at various ages. Jen smiles at photos of Adam kicking a football, riding a BMX bike, playing tennis, holding a boogie board at the beach. When she stops in front of a recent photo, where he's lost his hair and his tan and he sits in a director's chair as a game of backyard cricket takes place in the background, her smile slides away.

"That was last Christmas, playing cricket," says Adam. "I took a catch from that chair, got my cousin out for a duck. Remember that, Mum?"

"I sure do." His mother squeezes the juice of half a lemon into the bowl, starts tossing it through with a large slotted spoon. "Corey had a good whinge about that, acted like he was nine instead of nineteen. He always was a bit of a brat, that one."

"Yeah, he claimed it was a crowd catch so it didn't count. But we created a new position, called it Square Leg in a Chair." Adam laughs. "My uncles thought that was a great idea, they all grabbed a chair and sat down for the rest of the game too."

"With a beer, of course," adds his mother, sprinkling a handful of slivered almonds into the bowl.

"Well, of course ... we had Mid-Wicket in a Chair, Third Man in a Chair ... I suppose it should have been Mid-Wicket in a Chair with a Stubby."

"And Third man in a Chair with a Frothy," laughs Jen, walking back to the table.

"It's not really a laughing matter," says Adam's mother, bringing the serving bowl to the table. "They drink far too much, that side of the family." She grinds pepper into the bowl. "It'll catch up with them in the long run. I'd hate to see their livers." She spoons generous portions onto plates.

Jen sets the plates on their placemats. "Well, I suppose anything can happen to any of us, at any time," she says. "You could get run over by a bus ..."

"Yes, yes, you could get run over by a bus tomorrow," trills Adam's mother. "But nobody who says that thinks there's a snowflake's chance in hell of it actually happening."

Jen's lips stretch in a strained smile and she turns wide eyes on Adam. He shrugs and winks at her.

"Now what would you two like to drink, water or fresh juice?" asks Adam's mother.

"Just water," say Adam and Jen quickly, loudly, in unison.

11.00am Feed
by Claudia Bierschenk

While he drinks me empty, I empty glass after glass of water and think about food. Since he was born I have become a frequent visitor to most cafés in Berlin-Pankow and eaten: hazelnut-almond cake, peanut butter-chocolate cake, pear-chocolate tart, apple crumble, rhubarb crumble, brownies (walnut, chocolate, spelt, wholemeal), New York Cheesecake, Blueberry cheesecake, honey-and-nut cake, apple-cinnamon cake, poppyseed-muesli cake, coconut macaroons, rice-pudding cake, plum tart, goats cheese and apple sandwiches, gouda and pesto sandwiches with Hungarian salami, rye bagels with creamed goats cheese and fig mustard, sweet potato and chorizo quiche, sauerkraut and blood sausage quiche, countless ham and cheese omelettes. I have eaten avocados wrapped in thick slices of ham over the sink at four in the morning after a night feed. I allow myself one café latte a day, the ultimate indulgence. Any more caffeine and he'd never go to sleep. I stay away from onions and garlic because it would give him colic. And in weak moments I try to conjure up the warm, burning sensation of whisky trickling down my throat.

5.30am
New Haven, Connecticut, USA

Breakfast with Mandy
by Paul Beckman

Martin, up before his alarm rang, walked directly to his kitchen. He opened his refrigerator and took out two eggs, two slices of cheese, a green pepper, ketchup, butter and hot sauce. Today was his thirty-fifth birthday. He loved when his birthday came on a Friday because he took the day off and celebrated with a three day weekend.

He sliced open the two poppy seed rolls he'd purchased from the bakery while the skillet on his stove was melting the butter slowly. He cut off two sheets of aluminum foil and laid them out on the counter. With practiced hands he swirled the butter in the skillet and one-handed cracked the eggs, keeping the yolks intact. He buttered the rolls, placed them in a second skillet to crisp up and cut two slices of pepper. Martin took the rolls, lay them open on the foil and then he flipped over the eggs and dropped a slice of cheese on each and ketchup and hot sauced the rolls all the while keeping an eye on the eggs. He liked his eggs soft so the yolks would mix with the ketchup, hot sauce and cheese and coat the roll and then his mouth. He liked the feel of the squish of the yolk. Just as the cheese began to melt he turned off the burner and lifted each egg carefully onto the rolls and wrapped them.

He put them in his straw picnic basket along with a small milk carton and a juice box and then checked the window

65

thermometer to see what the temperature was this fine spring Friday. It was mid-thirties, as he expected.

Martin took a quick shower, brushed his teeth, combed his hair and dressed with a sweater and flannel shirt. He checked the time, donned his parka, grabbed the picnic basket and walked out into the early morning dark to his car. He sat listening to his Barry Manilow CD as the car warmed, the windows defrosted and *Mandy* began playing. He turned the stereo to repeat and drove off.

He drove around the corner and up the hill and parked his car, looking down at the apartments below, and as the morning light was breaking he opened his picnic basket, took out his sandwiches and binoculars and waited for the light to come on in Mandy Blanchard's bedroom.

He was halfway through his first egg sandwich, congratulating himself on how perfect the eggs were and how smart he was to add the crunch of green pepper, when Mandy's light turned on. He upped the volume and picked up his binoculars as the yolk ran down his chin.

Martin knew her routine and held the glasses with one hand and the rest of his sandwich with the other. He stuffed the last bite into his mouth and wiped yolk from his lips without taking his eyes from her opening the curtains wearing only a T-shirt. She looked up at the sky beyond him, stretched and yawned, her breasts tight against her shirt, nipples poking up towards the sky, and Martin had to hold the glasses with both hands as she then lifted her shirt off over her head and appeared to be staring right at him teasing him with her body. *Wow! Mandy's never taken off her top before, he thought. What a birthday present!*

Martin held on tight with his left hand, grabbed the next egg sandwich and chewed off a chunk in the middle. The yolk shot straight out onto the car window and as Mandy walked out of his sight towards the bathroom Martin tilted his seat to recline.

Bryndzové Halušky
by Andrew Stancek

"So she's been teaching me to cook, can you imagine? I'm not washing dishes or breaking plates, I'm making sauces and thinking I'll go to chef school and she's so – Are you listening to me at all? Are you here?" Ferko shoves him and David squints against the rain. Main Square, normally bustling with pedestrians, is deserted as they walk toward Michael's Gate.

"Yeah, yeah, I'm happy for you. You're living the happily ever after. I don't have a clue where Taia is. Three weeks. She said don't get in touch, never want to see you, go away. She has a new cell and at her parents' place, her father sicced the dog on me. He said he'll have me arrested for harassment and that he always knew I was a turd and it's my fuckin' fault they don't know where their baby is and maybe he isn't even lying. Yeah, I am happy you and Yolanda are together again, but ..."

Ferko looks over at David's scrunched face and sunken eyes. "Rough, I know. I've been on the streets, with her, without her. Doesn't help you, still, I know. We only have an hour before more invoices and stock-taking. Can't afford to be without the paycheck, as shitty as the job is. I'll buy you lunch this time. This place here, down this alley, their *bryndzové halušky* won't poison us."

"I can't eat. Can't. My insides churn, even when I force something down, I throw it up. I think of something I've always liked, like a sausage, or a *kremez* and by the time I start eating it ... It's in my head now, Ferko; I think I've had it."

Ferko holds onto the railing down the steps into the restaurant, inhales the sharp smell of bacon. "Right here, this place. They use real *bryndza*, not the pretend stuff, and yes, it's not May yet, so it's not the very best, but they know what they're doing. I've been making my own, with Yolanda supervising. Easy once you master it." Ferko pushes David along to a small table in the corner, signals the waiter for two portions. David stares at an embroidered linen hanging on the wall.

"I'm going to kill myself." He points at the Janosik figure in the embroidery. "He was hanged by the rib. Every Slovak school child knows that. But nobody else was hanged that way, ever. He was probably hanging forever, maybe ravens flew by and ripped off pieces of flesh. Look. Every folk artist for hundreds of years has portrayed Janosik standing full-face with his *valaska* axe, or sometimes robbing a carriage. But here, the hanging, and that bird, behind him, all colorful, is it a peacock or a phoenix? It's a sign for me, Ferko, a sign."

The waiter throws two plates in front of them, heaving with dumplings, cheese, bacon and grease on the sides. Ferko stares into the plate. "Eighty-seven kinds of bacon. Five basic ways of cubing it. Different species of *halusky*. Purists only use raw potato but some chefs use boiled and a few don't even use potato. Many cheat with inferior *bryndza*." He looks over at his friend. "You don't give a flying fuck, do you? I used to just eat but I now think about the how. With my grandma's cooking and my aunt's I always gobbled down seconds, thirds, fourths, more, more,

more. And now with The Woman teaching me, food is not the same."

Ferko digs in, makes a face when he burns his lips but continues talking and chewing. "David, she's not the only one. Snap out." From the table next to them, the linen napkin begins to rise. It flaps, grows a beak, red eyes that stare, sprouts feathers and a squat body with hooked claws. The beak smoothes the feathers while the beast spreads its tail fan and watches. It hops onto the table in front of David. Its squawk is guttural. It shakes its head, spreads its wings and flies low above the stairs and out. David watches the soaring wings. Ferko digs his fork into the dumplings.

5.30am
Fort Worth, Texas, USA

A Dash of Pepper
by Tom Fegan

A dash of pepper removed the flatness of the egg white omelet I had prepared for my early morning breakfast. Dry wheat toast and black coffee accompanied my efforts at a low fat and no fun diet. This along with cholesterol medicine changed my lifestyle as a divorced police detective grabbing junk food as sustenance.

I deliberated on my report to the District Attorney's office, regarding a two-year cold case in which a teenage tomboy named Gerry Day had been murdered and dumped in the trunk of her Chevrolet; stabbed to death but not sexually violated. Her billfold had been fleeced.

Evidence of defensive wounds, broken fingernails, bruised fists and torn clothing showed she fought with the assailant who had probably been waiting in the backseat for her. The vehicle had been found at a mall in Fort Worth. No one had seen anything. I cleaned my plate and sighed. This was my time to drink coffee and meditate.

There was blood along with a cigarette butt left in her vehicle. Gerry Day left her mother and father in mourning. She was admired for shunning girlie activities, but liked the boys. Her previous boyfriend had been interviewed but he too cried about her. "No one deserves that," he sobbed. I agreed. I had yet to see any homicide be justified.

Ben Tomlinson, a neighbor, had been arrested for a violent rampage the day following the discovery of Gerry Day. The twenty-year-old heisted a bicycle from a child at gunpoint, carjacked a vehicle while on the bike and robbed a convenience store. The manager shot Tomlinson in the leg as he escaped. While blood dripped from his leg he managed to floorboard the stolen vehicle and run down a pedestrian. The victim became wheelchair bound. Tomlinson had a history of mixing meth, pot and booze. His violence matched the murder. He was convicted and imprisoned for his actions but was never connected with the murder of Gerry Day.

The night she went missing her plans were to go to a friend's home, watch a movie and eat pizza. It could only be surmised the attacker moved when they were a few blocks away and forced her to drive somewhere private where the incident occurred. I set my coffee cup down and glanced at my wall calendar: April 24, Friday, and my tax filing had been done weeks earlier; the return cashed. I glanced at my watch; it was time to brush my teeth and head out of my apartment to find out where my investigation was with the D.A.

"This is your life Marcus Jonson," I sighed to myself as I drove on the freeway. "No donuts on the way to work." I settled for a bottle of orange juice. My sweet tooth kicks in when I am under pressure and this case had done that.

6.55am
Oakville, Ontario, Canada

Neon Pink Sign
by Cindy Matthews

Strings of muddy, pink flesh litter the damp walkway leading to the hospital. Rosy and wet, they remind me of shards of half-cooked roast beef. I completed my final culinary exam of the college semester a week ago and have been sidestepping horny worms ever since. I can't recall a rainier April.

A male teen walks ahead of me. He wears khaki shorts, the sort with the oversize pockets with Velcro fasteners. The kid is on the short side and the too-long hem kisses his knees. He rolls the waist band down to reveal plaid undershorts. He strides with care to avoid sidewalk cracks before he pulverizes a six-inch worm with the sole of his boot.

"Take that, you son-of-a-bitch," the boy says to no one in particular.

Today is my first day as a summer orderly. Training took place last Friday. We focused on WHMIS and what to do when we find an otherwise healthy patient unconscious or if someone tries to choke us. I'd rather work in the kitchen or alongside a dietician. Because I bombed the food poisoning question at the interview, I face a summer emptying bedpans and slipping dentures into old biddies' mouths.

I study the wiggle of the hips now ahead of me as I

approach the entrance of the hospital. Round, plump, supported on legs boasting a 32-inch inseam. She has the legs I like to imagine when I'm alone in the shower which is most of the time. The woman with the hips stops just shy of the automatic doors and turns to light a cigarette.

"What's got you so happy?" she asks me.

I don't let on that the swoop of her hips turns me on. I recognize the woman from somewhere but I'm not certain where. Maybe my mom's soap. I watch the woman suck the filtered end of the cigarette. Her chest lingers long enough to fill with smoke before it sinks a half-foot on exhale. I make an appreciative sound someone else might call a grunt. I think about when Mom found Dad's *Playboy* squirrelled under my mattress.

"Happy – your bre – my parents," I stammer. I take a deep breath. "My parents make me happy." My face flushes and I touch my chin to conceal an angry patch of pimples.

The woman laughs but what passes between us is a look that says she'd rather have her eyes removed without anesthetic than waste another minute with the likes of me. Now I see she's standing next to a geezer strapped into a wheelchair, his IV pole saluting from the rear. He clutches a cigarette between his ring and baby fingers. I'm tempted to ask what happened to his other fingers but I'm way too polite.

I smooth the fabric of my turquoise smock and step into the bustle of the hospital's main foyer. The elevator going up is full of people so I climb the stairs. I find my supervisor, Chad, sitting with his Doc Martens sprawled across his desk. He reviews his expectations for the day.

"Walk around, smile a lot, offer water, ice chips, things like that."

No mention of bedpans. I breathe out in relief.

"Sometimes all the patient wants is someone to hold their hand," Chad says. "And, remember, never get in the way of the nurses. If you know what's good for you, drop off a box of doughnuts for their break."

I want to ask Chad what kind of cologne he's wearing but worry he'll think I'm creepy.

Better keep myself busy and out of the way of the nurses for the next two and a half hours. Easy, I think.

I scrub my hands with antiseptic soap and warm water, then head down the corridor. I sneak a peek into each room I pass and randomly select 413. A rubber stopper beneath the door keeps it open. There are two beds. I stare at the one by the window. It's empty. Freshly made in fact.

"She died," says a voice from the first bed. A tiny finger points at the bed near the window. "Last night." Saucer eyes peer from a bald head engulfed in pillows. I can't figure out if the eyes belong to a boy or girl. I decide to stay a while. I sit on a hard-backed chair between the two beds. I fist my hands and set them on my lap. My hands are clammy.

"I'm Bryan," I say. "And you're?"

"Lana." When she pulls herself up, a groan erupts, like that sound grizzly bears make on those *National Geographic* specials. Lana glances over at me like I'm supposed to know what to do next. I'm drowning but I try not to let on.

"Kid died of cancer. Like me," says Lana. "She had kidney. Mine's in my bowel."

I gulp. My back stiffens.

"Your family around?" I say, changing the subject.

"Na. Dad's overseas on business and Mom can't handle that I'm dying."

I can't handle much more of it, either. I shuffle my feet back and forth and swallow.

"We can pretend you're my family," she says.

I don't even have a kid sister. Phlegm sticks in my throat.

Lana slides herself back up the mattress and collapses in

74

the nest of pillows. From where I sit, it's like she's wearing a halo. She leans her head a little toward me. "Can you do me a favour?" she asks. Her eyes scrutinize my face as if she's counting my zits. She has blue eyes with tiny flecks of yellow. They are blood-shot and sit deep in her skull. She holds my gaze too long and I fidget in discomfort.

Lana lifts a hand and beckons me with a crooked finger. I lean closer. She whispers, "I'm starving. Think you could score me a pudding cup?" Her warm breath leaves my ear sticky moist.

"Sure, for you, anything," I say.

How unjust of the hospital to forget that little kid's breakfast tray, I think. I'll have to remember to talk to Chad about it later during debriefing. I salute Lana from the doorway and back out of the room. I head down the corridor to fulfill the mission. Near the linen closet past the nurses' station, I come upon an abandoned food trolley. I check over my shoulder before turning my fingers into secret agents seeking something for Lana. I find curled fruit-cup lids, grimy napkins, and crusty cereal bowls. Finally I detect something under an overturned styrofoam cup. An intact piece of toast with the crusts sliced off. I lift it with a tissue and carry it with robin-egg care into Lana's room. Until a talon grips my shoulder.

"I should fire your sorry ass right now. What are you thinking?" my supervisor hisses. Chad's cologne smells of roses and sweat and I remember how I detest the scent of flowers on a man.

Chad's jaw chomps up and down. "Christ, Bryan. We talked about this at training. The critical nature of the neon pink signs," he says.

"How do you expect me to remember everything?" I say. "I just started."

"Three god-damned letters. I don't expect you to remember everything. Just the three most important fucking letters in the entire hospital. N-P-O."

As Chad speaks, I notice his teeth are razor-sharp, like mini-sickles. My palms turn to mush and a wooziness akin to hangover causes me to sway.

"You honestly never saw the sign?" Chad asks. "Come on." He drags me like a naughty puppy to Lana's room. Chad points at tape residue on the outside of her door.

"Somebody's just moved it, is all." He boots the doorstop to release the door. There, nestled in a dust bunny is the neon pink sign.

I wait for an apology.

Chad says, "You're transferred to another ward for the rest of the day. How long 'til you fuck that up?"

Sure beats a needle for lunch.

2.00pm
Cyclades Islands, Greece

Marida
by Lyn Fowler

Kostas turns off the putt putt outboard motor of the dinghy and we glide towards the island with a man standing on a rock waving and beckoning us.

We pull up alongside a small jetty. The man reaches out with sinewed arms and knobbly hands to grab the rope that Kostas throws towards him. He ties the rope onto the buoy where his own boat is tied. He lifts his broad sun-lined face from under the black wool peaked cap. His blue eyes twinkle. Old man of the sea or not, he is fit and well. He grabs our hands and helps us out of our dinghy onto the jetty.

The old man leads us along a rocky path towards a house. Glazed blue ceramic jars line the front, whitewashed wall of the house. A large wooden barrel stands in front of an open door and blackened pots and pans hang from a wooden post. It is an outside kitchen. We all introduce ourselves and the old man, Sestos, invites us to follow him. On the sunny side of his house is a garden with tomatoes and cucumbers scrambling along the rocky ground. I lean down to take a closer look and Sestos hands me a wicker basket. I pick four tomatoes and a cucumber.

"Please take more," he says, "you can take them home for eating later."

Sestos washes the harvested tomatoes in a plastic bowl of

water collected from the spring in the side of the rocky cliff at the back of his house. As far as I can see, the bowl is the only plastic article here. Sestos piles the tomatoes, a slab of fetta and some black olives on top of the wooden barrel so we can all help ourselves. Plates are not necessary; this is a picnic after all. The tomatoes are fleshy, firm and fluted. I segment one tomato and place a slice of briny fetta on top. It does not need anything else. It is the taste of the Greek islands. The islanders make fetta with the milk from the goats they keep. On this island, the goats clambering energetically up and down the rocks must make good milk.

From just inside the doorway Sestos brings out a small tin. He gently forks out small salted dried fish, locally known as marida, and that we know as whitebait. While we crunch on these morsels and nibble on black olives, Sestos ladles wine out of one of the blue jars into a ceramic jug. He then pours the wine into two pottery cups. We all share a few sips. The wine is white, sweet and surprisingly chilled. I feel blessed and euphoric and it is not just the wine. We are standing around a barrel lunching on the simple delights of the land and the sea.

As we are casting off Sestos' island home back to our boat, he promises to bring fish for our dinner tonight.

Breakfast
by Gloria Garfunkel

This is allegedly my sixth day in the hospital and my fortieth birthday, Friday, April 24, 2015. That is what the nurse tells me over and over as I repeatedly ask her and then forget.

"When is April?" I say. "Is it before or after June?"

"Here, honey, so you can remember."

The nurse pins the information to the wall, but the minute I look away I forget it. I could do this all day and it wouldn't stick. I am unmoored in time and space, like I've fallen into a black hole.

I am attempting to eat breakfast but can only tolerate the orange juice and the soggy fruit cup.

The nurse harps on me to eat just a little more, like my obese mother harped my whole childhood. It only makes me want to eat less. When the nurse is gone, I wheel my hanging intravenous lines to the garbage can and dump the scrambled eggs and toast so she will leave me alone.

I see her inspect the trashcan when she returns.

She looks at me and laughs.

"You think you can fool me, girl? I'm up to your tricks. You've been doing this the whole time you've been here."

"I have?" I say. "I don't remember."

"I know you don't, honey. I know."

"I'm a vegan anyway," I say. "I don't eat eggs."

She brings me more ice water. That fills me up.

8.30am
a small town, upstate New York, USA

Bread and Butter
by Susan Tepper

Cooked food is no longer an option in our house. He cheated on me, he only gets a sandwich. On white bread. I would have bought Wonder Bread but the market carries Pepperidge Farm. It killed me. I wanted his sandwiches as gummy as possible. Because he is the sole income earner right now, me just having had a baby, my shrink said I have to at least feed him. How or what wasn't discussed in the session.

I'm holding the baby to my side, red faced and squalling. A new baby, less than six weeks old living in a broken home. Too young to have a sit-down. A talking to. But this baby gets the picture because it never stops crying and fussing.

He comes in for breakfast wearing shorts and a T. "Are you fucking for real?" I say. "It's probably about 35 fucking degrees outside."

I now use fuck or fucking or fuck you, or some variation, in every exchange with him. Hate has a way of solidifying some things and breaking down others. I used to cook big dinners with all the trimmings.

I point at a plate on the otherwise empty table. "Here is your breakfast sandwich."

While he was showering, I took two slices of white bread and buttered them.

"You didn't toast them," he says.

"Oh, you want fucking toast!" I put the baby in the carrier then pull the buttered slices apart chucking them into the toaster.

"Jeez, now the toaster will be all slimy from the butter," he says. "Hi Baby." Leaning down to stroke her cheek.

I press my back against the kitchen counter crossing my arms. "Well that's a fucking shame about the butter."

He avoids looking in my eyes that always smolder now. Puts the toaster knob down twice and manages to burn the bread. "Now it's burnt," he says.

"Well, I could smell it fucking burning, why couldn't you?"

He actually looks hurt.

I sit down with my bowl of cooked steaming oatmeal pouring in the half and half liberally.

"Is there any extra?" He's fixated on my bowl.

"Not a fucking spoonful extra."

"Oh." Silently he chews his burnt toast. "When are we going to name the baby?"

"Never. This baby will grow up and choose her own name."

"Couldn't that cause psychological problems?"

"You mean worse than the fucking psychological problems you caused? And continue to cause? Just by being fucking alive? Is that what you mean?"

After his breakfast sandwich, he goes down to his office in the basement where he operates an employment placement service.

I give the baby a bottle to quiet her down. Then clean up the breakfast table. I toss his dirty plate in the sink. Mine goes into the dishwasher. That's another thing: I won't put his plates in the dishwasher. If we run out of plates, well, no fucking big deal.

*　　　*　　　*

The Baby finishes the bottle and poops. I change her diaper
then decide to vacuum. The noise blocks out her squalling,
and other things I would rather not think about. Like the
fucking that went on behind my back while I was cooking
those gourmet meals and entertaining his stupid business-
placement clients. The worst pack of losers I'd ever come
across. If you can't hold down a managerial position at
McDonald's, do you really expect to become a business
success? Last I heard, the guy was doing the same job for
another fast food chain.

Breaking Eggs and Calling Them an Omelet

by Walter Giersbach

The girl had been draped over the mailbox like Salvador Dali's Limp Watches, dripping down the blue paint. She was wearing a matching blue dress and he'd appraised her white buttocks, pushed out like two frozen supermarket chickens. Why was she on Hester Street imitating a pile of garbage bags at one minute after midnight?

"Hey!" He got no response, which worsened his already-foul mood. Mom's funeral service had been a downer and the rain was getting worse. Would better times ever return?

He poked her, on her hip above one of the chickens.

"Piss off," the garbage bag muttered.

"C'mon." He'd tugged at her. There was no good reason for doing a Samaritan on this stranger, except leaving her at the curb like castoff furniture seemed uncivilized. Two teenagers standing in the shadows a few doors away had probably smelled fresh meat.

He hoisted the woman up, zombie-walking her limp legs over to Rivington St. She was good looking, even smelled good as he'd dragged her into his first floor loft. Very good looking. That was motivation of sorts. Save the good lookers, he'd thought laying her on his bed. He headed into the kitchen space, his heels echoing in the empty loft, to pour himself a whiskey.

Then he forgot his scavenged woman and began drawing. Drawing opened doors to salvation, helping him forget the memorial, the church full of aliens, his brother who had flown in from Minneapolis after dredging up a sense of duty. Forget death, the terrorist attacks, Russian invasions, and random acts of horror every day now. He'd immerse himself in the plight of Lucy Dingo. She'd make Saltzman sit up and say, "Damn, Mikey, I didn't think you had it in you. A totally new slant on literature and art!"

His head had fallen to the drawing board and he dreamed of Lucy. There was trouble in Cambridge. Alexander, the fallen angel, was dead. The dwarves had freaked and run amok in Springfield. This was a job for Lucy. She wasn't dead. Just hiding out until the time ripened and the fullness found her.

"Who the hell are you and where am I?"

Mike raised his head and looked at the woman in the blue dress. His wind-up clock said 8:34 and already he'd been asked two questions at once. "Um," he started, "Rivington Street. I'm Mike. I rescued you. From the rain, the street where you were decorating a mailbox. And some teenagers that were eyeing you for dinner."

"You want me to say thank you? My knight in shining armor?" She pointed at his drawing board. "You're a goddamn starving artist. You guys can't even rescue yourselves." She sauntered around his loft touching shelves and tables, as though she had Helen Keller's sensory input in her fingers.

"You have a name?"

She turned. "Calliope Katsanakis. Most people call me Kelly."

"I'm going to make coffee. Want some?"

"What I really want to know is where's my pocketbook? You go through it and then dump it in a trash can?"

"Purse? By the bed, I think." He admired the fact that she didn't look hung over, that the dress emphasized her curves, that her tousled bed hair looked sexy in a B movie sort of way. Her breasts under the tight bodice of her dress resembled ripe apples, perhaps Golden Delicious. Be interesting to sketch her portrait as a still life of fruit, as Lucy Dingo incarnate.

"Comic books!" She laughed. "You draw comics!"

"Hey, I'm not peddling my ass on the street. Should have seen yourself last night. Too drunk to stand up and looking like a ten-dollar hooker. You coulda got in trouble."

"My ass is worth a lot more than ten bucks, buddy," and she stuck her face a few inches from his nose. "My apartment costs two large a month, I got a bank account and a retirement account, vacationed in the Bahamas two weeks ago ..."

"Excuse me for being a lowly artist, but I've published a graphic novel and even been reviewed in the *Times*." He inhaled the scent of perfume or hand lotion, surprised she didn't smell like a wet cat.

"Well, *la-de-dah*. So where's my coffee?"

"You insult me and then ask for breakfast?"

"You owe me. You saved my life, so according to custom – Chinese or something – you have to at least feed me."

He watched her wolf down bacon and an omelet, rip off pieces of toast, and wash down breakfast with orange juice and coffee.

"Thank you. Very good. So why's a grown-up drawing kids' comics?"

Mike drew a deep breath. "I said they're graphic novels. Comics were Donald Duck walking off the cliff. Suddenly realizing he's in mid-air, he drops a hundred feet and gets up with stars circling his head."

She glared, challenging him to go on.

"I weave words and art together to unravel the stuff of dreams. I can capture a gesture, a glance, a suggestive nuance. Make anything happen. Start an earthquake. Bring a new character back from the dead. Only the readers change, and they pay twenty-seven bucks for a hard cover edition of *Lucy Dingo*. It's an allegory of our dystopian culture – a better piece of reality, metaphorically speaking, than you give selling your ass."

"My ass is not an eleemosynary institution. It pays my debts."

Mike stared. "Where'd you learn that big word?"

"Bennington College. Twenty-six thousand bucks worth of college loans to prove it."

He squinted. "What kind of name is Calliope?"

"More coffee." She held out her mug. "The muse of poets, daughter of Zeus. Too much for your little brain? She taught Orpheus to sing, was the inspiration for Homer's *Odyssey*."

"So why are you hooking men when you have an education and" – he waved his hand airily – "could work in some ivory tower uptown?"

"I'm not a hooker. I'm a call girl. There's a difference. But my daytime job is none of your business. Not going to have you stalk in with ink all over your shirt asking me for a date."

"I don't think I'd do that." He considered the waves of paranoia that enveloped him each time he ventured north of

23rd Street. It was his agoraphobia, fear of the marketplace full of people, any place where anxiety overwhelmed him. "We're too different. See, you're taking the path of least resistance. Doing your nighttime workout knocking off out-of-town Johns to pay the bills. I'm trying to find deeper meaning. Categorize philosophical theses."

"The old existential meaning-of-life-crapola?" She cupped her chin in her hand and scrutinized him as she might a slab of meat in a supermarket. "I used to think about that a lot – when I was fifteen years old. No, you're ordering chicken nuggets at the banquet of life."

"The 'why me?' questions never go away, Calliope." He was snarling now. "My kid sister died of cancer last year. My dad ran off when he lost his job in the recession. My mom had a drinking problem and I was her go-to guy until the Social Security check arrived each month. Don't give me shit about fantasizing. I just draw the story boards and write the lines, looking for an answer, hoping there's someone out there who'll say, 'Yeah, I know what you're saying. I feel that way myself.'"

"Sorry about all that, but it was that philosopher Bergson or someone who said 'Shit happens.'"

"Thanks for your middle-class sarcasm, but I don't need it."

She stood slowly, ambled to the sleeping area and returned with her purse. Acting indifferent, she threw a bill on the table. "Here's a hundred. Should be enough to pay for breakfast. Sorry I don't do dishes."

He closed his eyes. "Just get out of here. I don't need your shit. I have stuff to do."

"What'd you mean, your mom *had* a drinking problem?"

"Just leave. Please."

She picked up her plate, glass and mug. "Know why I don't do dishes?" She walked to the sink and tossed them in.

Mike jumped as he heard china break. "Cause there's always more where those came from."

A minute later she slammed the door.

"Calliope," he said to the empty room. *Who was that Helen of Troy? Coming into his life and hijacking his artistic equanimity? Goddamn women. And now he was out of eggs and juice, too.*

Eating Disorder
by Gloria Garfunkel

A team of doctors arrive with their white coats and superior attitudes, prodding me like I am a specimen. I don't even know what kind of doctors they are. I think they are psychiatrists, neurologists, and just plain physicians. One is a doctor from my insurance company, who keeps saying I look so much better which I know he's just saying because I am an expensive patient and he wants me out of the hospital as soon as possible. He seems to be the only one who thinks this except for me.

"I want to go home," I sob. "Please let me go home."

"A few more days," they say. "Just a few more days." Then they do their quicky Mental Status Exam.

I try to guess what they are thinking, if I passed the test or not. I can't answer a lot of their questions. I have trouble speaking, finding the right words. My memory is terrible. I can't remember any of the strings of words they throw at me. I can't remember the day or date, as this seems like one long day. They ask me why I keep looking at the clock, and not at them and I say the clock is the only stable factor in my unmoored reality. My brain has been eaten by moths.

"How's the eating going?" one doctor asks. "The nurses say you are still hiding your food. We are thinking of sending you to an eating disorders program for two weeks after you are discharged."

"I don't have an eating disorder. I hate hospital food. And I'm ... um ... vegan. I can't count ... what are they called ... um ... calories. I won't be able to learn anything. You should send me to ... um ... a neurology day program. I need to learn how to think."

"Non-compliant," one doctor mutters to the other.

"You seem agitated," another says.

"You would be agitated, too, in my situation. I have a gigantic belly and look pregnant."

They glance at each other like I am psychotic. I can see it through their poker faces. The doctors insist I am too concerned with my weight, which is totally normal.

"I know that's a lie," I say.

They call me obsessive. Can't they see how bloated my stomach is, hidden by this hospital gown? Doctors can be so judgmental, ready to accuse you of a diagnosis like criminals with a crime. Eating disorder. God, I no longer have control of anything. At least I should be able to control what I eat.

The Mortician's Visit
by AR Neal

Bud's grin spanned his fleshy face. "Come on in, Willy!" He bellowed around the cigar tucked wetly in the corner of his mouth and pawed the mortician into the house. "Nancy! Willy's here!"

"I'm back here!"

"Willy –"

"It's William."

Bud gripped the other man's shoulder and lowered his voice. "Willy, William, whatever. Look, man, lemme talk to you." Bud and William had been in high school together; it was no mystery as to who bullied whom. "You know my sister don't have a lot of assets. I hope you gave her a square deal on this funeral."

William stiffened. "I need to speak to Mrs. Washington." He stepped around Bud and followed his nose to the kitchen. "Nancy," he said as took her hand and placed another of his business cards in it.

"Thank you, William." Nancy juggled the card from hand to hand as she wiped each against her apron. "Just look at you: 'Whipper Funeral Services' – I bet you made your father proud."

William had taken over the family business right after college and continued as the seventh generation of Whippers

92

in charge of final arrangements for most of the neighborhood. She tucked the card in an apron pocket.

"Please," she moved a tray of deviled eggs off a bar stool, "have a seat."

"Thank you." His eyes moved over plates of chicken, bowls of fruit, and assorted cakes and pies scattered across every tabletop, chair, and stool in the kitchen. "My but you've been busy," he commented, as Nancy handed him a biscuit and his stomach growled appreciatively. "Thank you; you make the best biscuits."

She winked. "I always make a few extra just for you when we have socials at the church."

He finished the biscuit in two bites and then looked her in the eye. "Are we all ready for today?"

"Doesn't it look like it?" Nancy waved her hand around the kitchen and laughed. "Daddy would be happy, I think."

William cleared his throat. "You mentioned that you wanted James as a pallbearer."

"Where are my manners?" Nancy walked to a cabinet and opened the door, revealing rows of neatly arranged mugs. "Would you like some coffee? I just made a fresh pot."

He shook his head.

"Everything all right up in here?" Bud asked as he shambled in, took a biscuit from a tray on the stool next to where William stood, and shoved it in his mouth. "You need any help, Nancy?"

"Bud! Don't talk with your mouth full," she said, handing him a napkin. "You are nothin' but a big child. Get out – William and I have business, and it's none of yours."

He took two more biscuits and smiled. "Okay, okay. I just want to make sure Willy's taking care of you right."

"Bud, I hear the doorbell. It might be your catered breakfast." Bud dashed from the kitchen as Nancy moved the tray of biscuits from the stool to the last clear place on the counter, beside the coffee pot, and then sat down. "I'm not sure James will be able to serve as a pallbearer," she said with a sigh.

"Right now we have Bud, Jamal, his friend Sam and three of Calvin's lodge mates," William said gently. "We'll be fine if James can't make it."

"I'm sure he'll be along. You sure you don't want any coffee?" William shook his head again. "Well," Nancy sighed, "I guess this is it, huh?"

He held her hand gently; it was the first thing he learned how to do as a mortician. "We'll take good care of Calvin." He paused as he thought about how much fun he used to have with Nancy, Bud, and Calvin when they were kids and played in each other's backyards." Your husband was a very good man, Nancy."

She smiled and wiped a tear. "You are a good man, William."

"I'm glad you think so, Nancy." He dropped his professional veneer for a moment as his own tears fell. He pulled a handkerchief from his inner pocket, blew his nose loudly, and said, "You always looked out for me, you know, with Bud when we were in school."

She nodded. "Bud really likes you; that's why he messes with you," she commented as they walked to the kitchen door. "Thank you for everything, William. Is there anything else you need from me? Daddy did a good job putting his things in order but I don't want to forget anything."

"I have everything," he answered. "The car will be here by 9.30 to carry you to the church and the viewing will start at 10.00."

Nancy walked him to the door, said good-bye and closed the door behind him. Turning around, she stepped backwards as Stella had walked right up behind her.

"Here, honey," her sister-in-law cooed. "I made you a plate." She had pulled together a plate of fried potatoes, scrambled eggs, grits, bacon, and sage sausage from Bud's order.

"That's okay, Stella. You know I'm not a fan of diner food." Nancy swallowed a laugh as Bud scowled. "Now Bud, I'm not sayin' anything you didn't already know," she said, giggling. She turned to Odessa, Jamal, Cora-Lynn, Stella, and several other relatives. "There's a casserole on the sideboard." Everyone except Bud hurried into the kitchen.

Bud snorted. "Don't nobody like your old-fashioned breakfast casserole. It's nothin' but leftovers anyway."

"Why you lyin', Bud?" Their older sister, Odessa, fussed as she returned with a heaping plate, a half-eaten biscuit on top. "Everybody *loves* Nancy's casserole. Hers was the only one Mamma would eat." She perched on the arm of a chair, swallowed the rest of the biscuit in one bite and continued talking. "And she hated that diner stuff you always get," she added, licking her fingers.

"I know that's right!" Cora-Lynn, their youngest sister, piped up, sitting down on the chair beside Odessa. "And even if Nancy put every leftover in the house in her casserole, I bet it would be more moist than that cardboard you bought." The two sisters erupted with laughter.

"Look, you all finish up and don't make a mess in here!" Nancy ordered. "I'm going to get dressed. The car will be here soon and we need to be right. This is Daddy's day."

The other women stopped laughing and Cora-Lynn wiped tears from her eyes as Nancy walked toward the stairway.

Bud stepped to the table to pull the aluminum foil covers back over the food he had purchased. He picked up the plate he had left on the arm of his chair and bit into a slice of bacon that crackled across the silence.

"That bacon is so old, Aunt Jemima cooked it!" Odessa joked, and the sisters broke into laughter again as Bud frowned.

"I know that's right," Nancy added, and laughed despite herself as she started up the stairs.

Kit and Czarina
by Kyle Hemmings

Kit is standing over a mixing bowl beating eggs and farmers cheese then adding the sifted flour, salt, sugar, and baking soda. She is making Czarina's favorite breakfast – *syrniki* – which resemble American pancakes, only shrunken. She turns the heat on a non-stick skillet, one she purchased on sale at a store going out of business, and places each log of cut-out dough in the oil.

It is the morning of Friday, April 24. It is slightly chilly and the sky is partly cloudy. That means there's hope for the sun to break through, thinks Kit, who is nineteen years old and wears her black hair in bangs and her frilly skirts with knee sox. From the window, Kit can hear a young man (who she pictures with curly hair and torn jeans) strum an acoustic guitar while singing a cover of Sam Smith's *Stay with Me*.

Czarina, who is sixty-something and a tattoo artist, hobbles to the small dining room table in the apartment overlooking East 6th Street. Lately, she hasn't been feeling well and depends on Kit to buy her medications from the Rite-Aid a couple of blocks over. Despite Kit's pleading, Czarina often cancels her appointments with the specialists. She does not trust doctors. "When it's your time to go, you are going to go anyway, no matter what they promise you."

The two women sit across each other and take the syrniki from the paper towel that has absorbed the oil.

"It is good," says Czarina, chewing her syrniki, "I'd hire you as my personal chef any day."

Kit takes a gulp of milk.

"And you can be my personal tattoo lady forever."

Czarina winkles her nose then smirks.

Czarina had taken in Kit because being a runaway from Spokane and with a dysfunctional family that would fight over the slightest thing, she had nowhere to go.

Kit wipes her mouth with a napkin.

"Are you still mad at me? I mean what we talked about last night."

Czarina dips her tea bag several times in an off-white porcelain cup, slightly chipped near the base. She folds the tea bag around a spoon with painstaking precision, and it must be snug. Kit offers her more syrniki. Czarina refuses.

"It's too late for me to get mad or stay mad. People never listen anyway. But you are living under my humble roof. And what you are doing is dangerous. You know, I have adopted you, more or less. Maybe more."

Kit's face flushes pink. She runs a finger around the rim of the empty glass, then pulls it up to her face to see a part of her reflection. She can't.

"Look," Kit says opening one hand out on the table as she speaks, "it's just something temporary. It's helping us pay the rent, helping to put me through dance school, helping to buy you medications. Maybe you forgot but you have no insurance."

Czarina plays with some flakes of the syrniki then pushes the plate away. She turns her face. The corners of her lips press deep into her chin.

"But you don't have to sell yourself like ..." She looks down at the remaining syrniki in the paper towel. "Like hotcakes."

Kit is tempted to giggle.

"It is my body and I'm only in it for the money and it's helping the both of us survive."

Czarina lowers her head, shoots Kit a piercing stare. A smile slowly makes it way across her face.

"We could get by without you exposing yourself to all kinds of dangerous men."

"I told you it's only temporary. And what's so funny?"

"I was thinking of this old boyfriend I once had when I moved to the East Village. He taught me this ancient method of tattooing. It used to be practiced in Japan. He used this bamboo stick like a pool cure and he stabbed my back with ink."

"Did you like the tattoos?"

"I was never sure. But I was in love with him, he was dangerous."

Kit rests her chin on her palms. Her eyes twinkle. "Let me guess. He was a Japanese gangster."

Czarina laughs with a raspy sound.

"Yes. Yes he was. But he was good to me. Taught me a lot about tattooing."

Kit and Czarina stare at each other across the table.

"Are you sure you're full?"

Czarina rubs her belly. "Oh, very much so, dear girl."

"Well, listen. I'll promise you something if you promise me something."

Czarina's rolls her head to one side. Her dark eyes glisten. "Is it a bribe?"

"Sort of. I'll give up hustling if you tattoo my back."

"You not hustling would be the best thing you could give me. What would you like me to tattoo on your back?"

"Every dish you taught me to make since I've been here."

Czarina offers a slow wide grin. "And why?"

"So in case one of us has to leave, I'll have something to remember you whenever I look over my shoulder in the mirror."

"The menu might make you hungry."

Kit gathers the plates and silverware and washes them in the kitchen. Czarina hums a song that Kit does not recognize.

Later, in the back room, she removes her shirt and lies face forward on a long red cushion. Czarina begins the precise lettering.

"Do you know what I want to tattoo on your skin?"

"What?" says Kit, craning her neck back.

"Bad girls need love."

"And more doctor visits." Kit giggles.

It takes Czarina most of the morning to complete the menu. She is fanatical about spacing and correct spelling. When she is done, she says, "Your menu is ready."

Kit reaches out with one hand and takes Czarina's.

"You're a good mother," says Kit.

"You're my only child," says Czarina.

Tea for Two
by Gill Hoffs

"A pot of Earl Grey for two, milk on the side – in a jug if you have it, not those fiddly plastic things, and a slice of chocolate cake with two forks."

The order's familiar, the café less so. He doesn't come to town that often, not this part of it anyway, but the place seems nice enough and the wipe-clean menu sheets have indeed been wiped clean and there are other old farts at Formica tables avoiding April showers or the loneliness of home. He doesn't feel out of place here like he does in the logoed coffee shops with their surly speed and expectations of you picking up a new lingo just to order. If he wanted to speak Italian he'd bloody go there.

The place smells of fried onions and bacon, well done toast and instant coffee. It's long past lunchtime but is it teatime? His stomach could do with a little something but not a full plate. Nothing savoury yet. He looks across the table at her wrist, trying to read the face of the gold watch she wears for 'going out', the one he gave her for their fiftieth, but of course it isn't there. *She* isn't there. And her absence crushes his throat all over again so when the waiter lays a serviette and fork at his elbow he can't speak to say, "I'm sorry, I made a mistake, there'll be no-one joining me." The sorrow swells his tongue and his eyes blink.

When the teapot arrives, white and nothing fancy, he's recovered enough to mumble "Thanks" to the boy without adding any kind of comment on his tattoos. The lid slips as he pours them both a cup though she isn't there and never will be, steaming his glasses and scalding his fingers, and since she's not there to tell him off he mutters "Fucker" then feels guilty. The chocolate cake arrives as he swirls milk in their cups with a flourish, more in his than in hers, and he resolves to drink them both and eat the lot even if it makes him queasy.

Most people in here have bags beside them on the table or chair or knocked over on the floor at their feet. He can tell who's been to the library (crumpled carrier bags showing signs of regular re-use and sometimes the straight creases of folding), who's been to the library for something they're a bit embarrassed about (flimsy zipped carryall in black or navy), and who's been shopping "for bits" as Marie called it.

He has a letter in his coat pocket beside the folded Kleenex she insisted he carry at all times, and half a pencil. Or perhaps it still counts as just 'a pencil' even when it's whittled down to a stub? So long as the ratio of core to covering is the same it must still – he is prattling, and even when it is entirely internal, it irritates him. He directs his attentions to the cake.

Instead of forking the thin end of the wedge and leaving Marie to attack the icing he inserts the fork between the layers and levers the slice in two. Does he really need to eat it with a fork? Does anyone care? He picks up a layer and bites into it, the chill of refrigeration spreading through his tongue and teeth. Best not to think of the cold, or refrigeration.

The solicitors' office had been cold, too. A secretary had been complaining to the receptionist about the heating going off at Easter when he arrived for his appointment. He'd tried to join in with the banter, get back to normal like, but she exited the room without a word when he remarked, "The cold should help you burn off all them Easter eggs." The red in her cheeks should keep her warm for a bit at least.

He hadn't considered Marie leaving a will, they'd both assumed since he was the older and unhealthier that he'd be going first. They'd had life insurance sorted since his forties and he'd given her his blessing should she want to flirt or even remarry. After today's meeting and the solicitor – the senior partner, no less – shaking his hand and solemnly assuring him his wife had left him well taken care of (she always did), he could have gone somewhere fancier for a cup of tea. Somewhere with bone china and fabric tablecloths and the menu in a leatherette folder and a fresh carnation on the table. Maybe even a sign near the door telling patrons 'Please Wait To Be Seated'. But a lifetime of careful enjoyment cautioned him to stick to what he knew, at least for the time being. And without Marie, there would be no fun in such extravagance.

He watches the waiter as he wipes a nearby table, lifting the salt and pepper pots and menu and checking the chair-seats for crumbs. A proper job of it, no cutting corners. He'll leave him a right good tip, a proper cash one, not a note telling him to get his hair cut or owt like that.

After he finishes the first cup of tea, the one with extra milk, he tries more cake. The stodge is sickening but he hasn't the stomach to try her tea yet so he carries on. Waste not, want not. Or waste not, waist not, as Marie would say with her hand on his belly. He's crumbling the cake into a smeary mess when the waiter appears at his side.

"Stood up?"

"Eh?"

The lad gestures at Marie's empty chair with a dishcloth. "She still at the sales?"

"Oh. Um, no. Meeting me later, she's been held up." Which is kind of true, at a stretch, if you believe in the afterlife. He's not sure that he does but he'd like to.

He stands up, zipping his coat and making a show of getting his collar right while the boy takes the hint and walks over to the till. He tucks a couple of pound coins from his pocket under the edge of the plate, out of sight of potential pilferers, and gets his wallet out to pay, edging past old biddies leaving the loo. It's only when he hands over a fiver that he notices the tips teacup beside the cash register and briefly debates whether to double tip to avoid looking stingy. If Marie was there she'd smile at the boy and tell him he'd find a little something for his trouble on the table, but it's too soon for smiles of any sort so he stares out the window instead. A *Big Issue* seller meets his gaze, clutching her magazines to her chest as rain trickles off her umbrella. Nobody stops to buy one as he stands there, receiving change with a full belly and the guilty conscience that comes with fresh grief.

"How much is it for a meal here?"

The boy fumbles a menu from beside the till. "Depends what you're having and when, though we do a pensioner special on Wednesdays before 3.00. If you're struggling come by late on when we're clearing up –"

"Would a tenner cover something like an all-day-breakfast, tea, and a pudding? Just now, I mean?" And his fingers find one in his wallet, automatically stroking the photo of Marie while they're in there.

"Sure, and probably some change."

She looks cold out there. Maybe twenty, tired and damp and spring-shower cold. He hands over the money. "Give her a good feed, will you? Let her sit and get a wee heat. Tell her it's a present from Marie."

He nips to the toilet, bladder not what it was, and washes his hands with squirty soap that smells of mango for longer than usual before he leaves. A check in the mirror above the sink shows the folly of eating chocolate cake with fingers instead of a fork. Mopping his face with wet toilet paper he notices new wrinkles but fuck 'em, no-one else is going to care if his face looks like an elephant's scrotum or is covered in crumbs. When Marie pointed out a stain on his sweater or smear on his face he always protested at the clean up, and claimed he was saving a snack for later. He gives up on his face before the tears come.

Leaving the toilet he sees the girl from outside now seated at the window near the door, hands round a mug of what looks like hot chocolate unless she's someone who likes coffee topped with marshmallows, sprinkles, and a cornet of whipped cream. With her hat off she looks younger than he thought. He walks past her table to the door and is almost away when she says, "Pass my thanks to Marie, will you please?" with the same soft lilt as his girl when they started courting, and the tears come: he is undone.

Escaping the café, he's grateful for the rain.

10.30am
Acton, Massachusetts, USA

Huge
by Michael Webb

I stare at my reflection until my eyes, huge in the mirror in front of me, start to water. I close them, a tear gathering in one corner. I will it not to fall, not to etch a streak through the makeup I have just finished applying, and after a second or two, it doesn't, somehow disappearing, probably onto a lash or something. This is the last bit of silence and solitude I'm likely to get for the rest of the day, and I breathe it in with the air, enjoying not hearing my name, or the grotesque shortenings and nicknames they all use, loving the absence of tugs and pokes and grubby hands on my legs and my back and my face. I am still recovering from being yanked out of sleep – 10.30am is pretty late, but not when you didn't fall asleep until 4.

They're coming. From across three states, driving in the dim light of the false sun on a cold day, they come to the dead lawns and dead faces of Acton, Massachusetts. Too many people for our house, but my mother can't say no to anyone, and so they file in, uncles and aunts and cousins and boyfriends and girlfriends and brothers and friends and lost souls who had no plans, gathered in. And food, appetizers and chips and alcohol and juices and water and ice and multi-colored spills on the carpet. Then roasts and salads and side dishes and desserts and groaning platters of all kinds, excess of a sickening, crushing kind that nauseates me already, hours before it starts.

The words will start, coming at me from all corners, "Why aren't you eating?" and "Are you sure you should be eating that?" and "Tell me about school!" and "Are you thinking about college?" all that I have to bear up under silently, grinning, giving nice, safe answers that everyone will report back about how well adjusted I am. A full day of lying, saying what I am supposed to because heaven knows the worst possible thing is that we lose face in front of the family. The prospect exhausts me.

I dress carefully, trying to straddle the line between girl and woman, trying to appear unthreatening and safe, feminine, but also comfortable for the games I will wind up playing on the floor, Barbies or monsters or trains or schoolbus or Wild West. I can't stand the adults and all their questions and all the noise and the sports on the big screen, and I can't stand the teenage cousins who will try to look down my cleavage while they wait to play their videogame splatterfests. I don't fit in anywhere, and I will eventually end up wandering off, little hands in mine, away from the raucous mess and the smells and the constant eating.

I will wind up in my bedroom, clothes and pens and sharp things out of reach, playing with the smallest children because their games and their needs are the simplest, and I feel a crying need to be simple, to not be friend or girlfriend or daughter or student, to only be required to have a lap and refill a cup of juice and know a nursery rhyme and be able to read the book about the dog party. They are my salvation, their joy the only part of this enormous ritual that gives me any pleasure at all.

Clock Watching
by Gloria Garfunkel

I feel like I am somewhere out of Kafka. They torture me with inedible food when I'm not even hungry.

There are big windows with a nice view of rich people's houses, if you like that kind of thing, but I keep my shades down. My eyes hurt. They are never shut. I can't sleep. I watch the clock day and night, through 2.00am, 4.00am, 6.00am. Also, at night, in the dim light, I watch the ceiling move like the gentle rocking of a lake. Fixtures on the ceiling seem to constantly transform. It entertains me all night. I don't mention this to the doctors because they don't ask. They just ask if I have been seeing things that aren't there. I know the ceiling and fixtures are really there, they're just moving. Perceptual distortions, not hallucinations. I learned that in school.

I rely on the large clock on the wall day and night. It is my TV, as I can't stand watching real TV. The noise and action are too confusing and irritating and I can't follow the plot or even the sentences. I can't focus on anything for any length of time. Things just sweep through my brain, leaving no trace, like tiny grain moths fluttering by. The clock is always there. I can always check the time. Its movement is slow, like my thinking, but still seems fast enough for entertainment. I can follow its trajectory round the clock.

108

"Would you like some Ensure?" some nurse asks me in the middle of the night, maybe 3.00am. "You aren't sleeping anyway and you need to eat. Maybe if you had something in your stomach."

Right. Good try.

Tea for One
by Gill Hoffs

No-one at the window. No-one at the door. Bulbs she'd planted flowering pretty and unpicked in the garden, curtains exactly as he left them, and nothing but spiders scuttling within the cold dark house that had been their home. And when he gets to the door, no keys in his pocket.

"Fiddlesticks," then, louder, because she isn't there to hear. "Fuck fuck fuckity fuck."

Marie had always carried a set in her bag or the pocket of the heavy red wool coat he gave her one Christmas. Her 'Mrs Claus' coat as she called it, the one that meant he could refer to her as a scarlet woman while they were out at whist drives or meeting their son in Morrison's for a meal after they'd completed their weekly shop, their way of thanking him for a lift home with the messages and just staying in touch with them when they knew from unhappy friends that grown children often don't. He'd have to call him for the spare.

He checks his watch: half four. He'd be unreachable until five at least.

The rain comes on heavier and he doesn't like his neighbour's dog, a slavering incontinent beast with ridiculously enormous balls and a greying muzzle, so he shuts the gate and starts retracing his steps to town again.

He could buy somewhere else to live if he wanted. Somewhere closer to his son, or in the heart of town where the constant noise of traffic will distract him from the silence inside. Somewhere bigger or smaller, more modern or like his mum and dad's when he was a boy. The funeral director had said generally it was best to wait at least two years before making any big decisions, like giving up the family home, until the bereaved adjust to their loss and settle into their new role of the one left behind. But everywhere he walks inside, every drawer he opens, every piece of clothing he wears or washes or throws out reminds him he is on his ownsome. He might as well be somewhere more comfortable, where he doesn't have to trundle up the stairs a dozen times a day just to pee, and be miserable there instead.

The *Big Issue* seller's gone by the time he reaches the café again. The boy's wiping down the last few tables, menus too, when he walks in and asks, "Did anyone hand a set of keys in?" Just in case it isn't forgetfulness that's left him locked out.

"Sorry, no." The boy stops what he's doing and looks him over. "Is it definitely here you lost them? I've not done the loo yet, give me a second and I'll check in there."

He shakes his head. "You're alright, lad. They're likely at home, I thought I'd best check though." It's warm in here, pleasantly so, and his stomach grumbles aloud.

The boy points to a table near the till. "We're closing up but if you want a seat while I sort the place out for tomorrow you're welcome to a cup of tea and the last of the bacon if you fancy it. It's only going in the bin anyway."

He thinks about it, hungry, but not one to take charity. "Don't you want it?"

The boy shakes his head. "I had some for my lunch, I don't think I could face it. You'd be doing me a favour. The smell of it in the bin drives the foxes wild."

He agrees and sits, pulling out his mobile and squinting at the screen as the boy brings a blue plastic tray to the table laden with a mug of milky Earl Grey, red and brown sauce, and a fat bacon sandwich. The rind is brown and crispy, exactly as he likes it, and since Marie's not there to tell him to cut the fat off ("your arteries'll thank you if your trousers don't") he savours every mouthful. The mug warms his hands as the smell of bergamot mixes with the bacon-y aroma and his stomach sends a belch upwards that he doesn't quite manage to mute in his throat. The boy's putting chairs upside down on tables by the door and doesn't appear to notice, not that he necessarily cares if he does, he's just used to somebody reacting.

He checks his watch: five past five. Might as well call him.

"I forgot my keys again, son. Any chance you might come by and let me in?"

Was that a sigh? It sounded like one.

"I've another meeting still to go before I can leave for the weekend. We're off to Callie's parents' house for a few days, remember? I need to get everything sorted here before I'm off and it's a pretty tight schedule. Where are you?"

"In a café off the High Street, near the solicitors'. They're closing now, the boy let me in for a heat. When do you think you'll be here?"

"Seven thirty at the earliest. Sorry, Dad. Is there anywhere you can go in the meantime?"

He thinks of his neighbour's dog and the stink of her house and how unclean he feels after sitting on her sofa and its many tiny wet patches. "So that's me on my ownsome till half seven, eh?" He means it to come out in a jokey way but even to his ears it sounds desperate. "Only kidding, son, I'll be fine. I like a walk and I can take a look in the magazines

112

section at the shops for a bit. You'll give me a ring when you're setting off?"

The boy's at his elbow as his son starts to answer, saying "Excuse me –" while his son mentions work. "Hang on a second son, the boy wants a word with me."

"I couldn't help overhearing what you said. You can come back to mine till your son's free if you like? I only live a few minutes away."

He can hear his son saying, "What's that? What's happening?" and it's all a bit much after so much silence, so he hands his phone to the boy and says, "That'd be grand."

The boy blinks at him for a second then talks into the mobile, "Hello?" "Yes, I run the Hobgoblin on Pewterspear Road. I only live on the next street and your dad's welcome to come and wait with me. It's been really wet here and I don't want to send him out in the cold with a wet jacket if he'll be out again for a while." "Sorry, yes, I'm Alan, Alan Newall. It's the flat above the Jaded Dragon, opposite the cardshop. Press the button for 1B or call your dad if you want to stay with your car." "No, it's fine, he can keep my cat occupied while I sort some dinner. Yeah, will we say eight-ish then? I know, I heard about those roadworks on the radio, best not to rush."

He hands the phone back, smiles, and moves towards the kitchen.

"You sure about this Dad?"

He can hear the tiredness in his voice. "Yes, I'm sure, it'll be fine. I'd rather a cat than a pissy old dog any day of the week. I'll see you in a bit, son."

He never knows quite how to end a call to his son, he used to hand the receiver to Marie for a word then she'd smack a kiss down the line and finish with a "Love you son" so he's still holding the handset when the boy comes back with a leather jacket on and starts turning the lights off. The quick "Bye" from his son doesn't sit right with him but it'll have to do, especially since the line's now dead.

"Shall we head off then? Leave the dishes there, I'm opening up in the morning, I can take care of it then."

He struggles to his feet, his legs clearly reluctant to bear his weight, and tucks the phone back in his pocket. "Right you are, lad. Thanks for taking me in."

"No problem. Clarice loves company."

"That your girlfriend?"

The boy's smile tells him that's highly unlikely. One of those then.

"She likes to think so. A touch too furry for me, and her breath smells of fish."

"So long as she's got a working bladder, that's good enough for me."

Cloistered
by Cindy Matthews

Due to my early morning fuck-up as a summer orderly on the paediatric floor of the hospital, I find myself sitting across from Bob, a patient in psych. My supervisor, Chad, transferred me after I almost offed a kid by feeding her toast.

"Here's your chance. Don't mess it up," Chad had said before I headed for the ward. "Look me in the eyes and promise. Don't even think of mentioning fire to this guy."

That won't be so hard, now, will it? I think. "Chad, is there anything else I need to know about Bob, you know, for his and my safety?"

"Suffice to say if Bob messes up at the hospital, next stop for him is jail."

A flash went off inside me when I realized how fascinating working with Bob would be.

I pick up my cup of coffee and take a sip. Bob has Coke. I set a sleeve of saltines on the table for us to eat later. Bob and I are all alone in the recreation room. A voice like Bobby Darrin's oozes from a ceiling speaker. Light rain splatters against a nearby window.

"My first semester at culinary college I pulled dish pig duty during the President's banquet," I tell Bob. "It's an annual charity event where the hoity-toities pay $200.00 a plate to suck back smoked salmon, jumbo shrimp, crab legs, and cold soup."

"I don't like my soup cold," Bob says. Bob's about fifty. His hair is sparse and his remaining strands are grey and combed over.

"After the dignitaries left, the chef made us eat the leftover crab. 'It never keeps,' he said. 'I don't want to see a speck of it tomorrow. You hear me?' I hadn't eaten crab before and was afraid I might not like it. So, I hung back to stack the last of the plates in the sterilizer."

"I don't believe in eating seafood," Bob says. He chews an edge on his thumb.

"Jo-Anne, an exchange student from Ireland I'd taken a liking to, begged me to come over and try the crab. 'You'll love it,' she screamed. 'Leave the dishes. Come on, Bryan.'"

"I never worked in no kitchens before," says Bob. Old acne scars pit his face. I expect my pimply skin would result in skin like that one day.

"After I rotated the sterilizer dial, I slipped over to the walk-in coolers, and sat on a stool next to Jo-Anne who handed me a crab leg. We cracked, twisted, and wrenched to release slivers of white meat." I leaned hard against the back of the chair, looked directly at Bob, and belched.

"Soon, threads of meat and butter greased my fingers, wrists, and palms. You could have wrung us out," I say.

"I'm not fond of being sticky," says Bob. He takes a sip of his soft drink. "Unless I'm sharing a chocolate bar."

"Within minutes, my lips started buzzing and I was zooming to outer space. I was gonzo."

"Never was one for outer space," says Bob. He chews the other thumb and makes sucking noises that sound like wet farts.

"I ran to wash the crab off. Only I couldn't manage the god-damned taps on account of my greasy fingers. I started pawing at paper towels and the toilet paper roll but it was too late. I collapsed on the floor right by the toilet."

"Bet you didn't much like that," says Bob.

"Ambulance brought me right here, Bob, right to this very place," I say, tapping the table, "to the emergency department of the same hospital where I now work as a summer orderly. Cool, eh?"

"That is a very nice, circular kind of story," he says.

"Except I almost died, Bob. You get that part, right?"

Bob stands and walks over to refill his Styrofoam cup with ice and Coke. He shuffle-walks back to the table. His lips mouth words, as if he's choreographing, breaking down the mechanics of placing one foot behind another.

"Now I wear an Epipen. See." I lift my smock to reveal my fanny pack with two auto-injectors of epinephrine.

I push myself up and head for the games shelf near the bank of windows. I select a deck of cards and a cribbage board.

Back at the table, I hand Bob the cards. He struggles with shuffling. So he tosses the deck across the table and smooshes the cards around like a game of Pick-up sticks. When finished, he blows air hard over his lips and smiles.

"I've got a story for you, Mr. Big Shot Orderly," says Bob. "When I still lived with my family I gave myself time-outs. In a closet in the basement."

I deal six cards to Bob and six to me. Bob takes a few minutes to decide which two cards to place into my crib. At this rate, we'll still be playing our first game at shift change.

"Aren't time-outs more of a thing for kids, Bob?" I ask. His glare is so mean the hairs on my arms stiffen.

Bob says, "It got so I liked it more in the closet than being upstairs."

I set a five down after Bob's ten. "Fifteen two," I say. I move a peg along the cribbage board.

"Truth is, I'm not a fan of people," Bob says.

"Not so different than a lot of folks," I say.

I want to tell Bob I know about him and his family. Only I can't on account of me promising my asshole supervisor I wouldn't bring up the word *fire* with Bob. I wait to speak while Bob clears his throat.

"Nice double run for eight," I say. I point at the two eights, a seven and a six sitting in front of him. A gob of spittle trickles over his cleanly shaved chin. "See how I got that?" I ask. He doesn't say.

I run fingers through my hair and wait. The ticking of a clock on the wall opposite is deafening. When I look at Bob, his lips are tight, horizontal stalks of celery on a cutting board.

"Last time I went to the closet, I stayed a whole week," Bob says.

I wonder if he'd sooner shit his pants than leave that closet. I sip my drink but it's taken on that bitter taste stale coffee gets.

"The basement isn't finished. The wife used to nag me something fierce about that." He licks under his nose like a dog with a runny snout. "She left me no choice."

I rake the cards in and shuffle. I look up to see Bob has tugged a cribbage peg out of the board and perched it on his bottom lip.

"That old closet is where we kept junk. Broken skis, smelly running shoes, a bunch of baseballs, and those wooden badminton rackets."

Rackets make perfect kindling, I think. I stitch my lips into a line. I itch to bring up the fire. But I mayn't so I shuffle faster and faster to keep myself distracted. My father would say, "Watch you don't rub the tits off the queens."

"Door's got no slats so once it's closed, that's it. It's pitch black," Bob says.

For a second, I don't follow. There's too much going on. "You done playing?" I ask. He nods. I centre the deck on the table. Bob grabs the cards back like they'll grow legs and run off.

Bob spits out the peg and replaces it with a playing card. His lips maul the edge of the card, working the card's rim like he's nibbling corn on the cob. I reach over and retrieve the other cards from his steely grip. He fires the gnawed card at me. Using his teeth, he picks at the cuff of his hoodie. The edge of the card is moist, like a barely-peed diaper. The unlucky King of Hearts has a row of puncture marks lining his head.

My fingers tighten around the deck. The King is tacky and sticks to his neighbours. I open the sleeve of saltines and offer the package to Bob. He takes two, stacks them like a cracker sandwich, and attacks both at the same time.

"I don't much care for the dark," says Bob, specks of cracker sputtering from his lips.

"Most people don't," I say.

Crumbs of dried saltine collect in the corner of Bob's mouth. Bob looks as if he's asleep with his eyes open. His head lolls toward a shoulder. He has that look people on the subway get – a stare so piercing it causes everyone to shudder.

His teeth find the cuff again. For a moment, he stares at me like he's unsure how we met. When Bob looks over at the bank of windows, he squints against a flicker of sunlight. The earlier rain has finally stopped. Bob slouches in the chair. He pats his chest like he's looking for a pack of smokes and a lighter. I glance at the wall clock, its second hand grating in my ears.

Suddenly he pushes the table at me and says, "I've nothing to say about the fire."

Bob trudges to the vending machine. I follow a few feet behind. He stands in front of it, rocking from side to side, studying it like he's coaxing it to spit out free food.

I pause next to Bob. There's a pile of coins in my scrub pocket. I fumble with the change until the jingling drowns out the ticking clock. Bob's taller than I expect, over six feet in his slippers. He chuffs through his big teeth.

"Oh, look, Bob. Why don't we split a Mars bar?"

The yelp he releases sends a shiver through my spine.

Poison
by Gloria Garfunkel

Apparently I was hospitalized for a medication overdose which was not a suicide attempt but a mistaken double dose for a month with a very toxic drug by my incompetent psychiatrist, Irena Akanov. I want to sue her because she's ruined my life but my husband says it's not worth it. She caused a brain injury which will supposedly heal over time, maybe a year, but they can't predict how long or whether it will heal completely. I can't spell, do math, or remember a string of numbers like my phone number. I can't dial it even when it is tacked to the wall. I don't know if nine comes before or after eight. I can hardly find words or talk in sentences that make sense. I can't concentrate on reading and when I forced myself today to read *The New York Times* that they send around, I struggled to remember any tiny details like a headline or the date.

My doctors say that my brain had been injured by the medication and my husband told me they had called Poison Control while I was in the emergency room. This means I've lost my job and will have to get onto disability. Actually, I hate my job at Orwell Industries' Hospital where I typed dictated doctors' notes. It was so boring that I lived on coffee to get through the day. There is nothing entertaining about those notes. Physicians are terrible writers. The one good thing that has come of this disaster is that I never have to go back to Orwell.

Normally after work I make dinner for the kids and when they go to their rooms to play Warcraft on their computers until all hours, I write short stories and have been working on a novel. What will I do without words? This is the biggest tragedy of all.

The nurse (I can't remember their names) says I must eat more. But I never have an appetite, especially when served hospital food. The salmon last night had the texture of rubber, like those fake plastic foods and vomit they sell in joke shops. It practically bounced when it accidentally fell on the floor, like it was alive.

When the nurse asked about it, I said, "Well, it just fell. Anyway, I'm a vegan. I don't eat fish."

The nurse had agreed to order me a salad. It was drenched in dressing.

"I don't eat salad dressing either. I'm allergic to fat."

The nurse insisted that I drink a can of Ensure, that high calorie glop they give to anorexics. She watched me until I finished the whole can which seemed to take a couple of hours by the clock.

6.00pm
Berlin, Germany

6.00pm Feed
by Claudia Bierschenk

Each feed seems endless. He's latched on to me like an octopus. One little hand flails uncontrollably. A small fist bangs against my collarbone. Tiny fingers cling to my shirt. He doesn't know yet that these hands are part of his body. When he's full, he un-docks abruptly. Little mouth slightly open, a thread of milky saliva bridging his lips. Then he opens his eyes, looks at me, almost bemused, as if to say, "Oh, *you're* here, too?"

12.00noon
a small town, upstate New York, USA

Bread and Peanut Butter
by Susan Tepper

When the twelve o'clock whistle blows he comes back up the basement stairs, per usual, for his lunch. He wears a sheepish look. I think about calling him Lambchops but he might get the impression that I'm weakening. That I will whip up a rack of rosemary lamb. No such luck.

"Ready for lunch?" I say. I've got the baby again, clutched to my one side.

He looks doubtful, scratching his chin. "What is there?"

"Bread."

"Just bread?"

"I could spread on a little fucking peanut butter."

"I don't like peanut butter."

"I don't like fucking fucking."

He sits at the table. "OK."

I put the screaming baby back in the carrier and take the loaf and remove two slices. Smear on a thin layer of peanut butter. Jiffy. The cheapest the market sells.

"Jiffy? I like the other brand, what's it called? Smuckers?"

Smuckers like fuckers? I suddenly want to throw the Jiffy jar against the wall. "What fucking other brand?" I bang the Jiffy down on the table. "What fucking other brand? Do it yourself." I scoop up The Baby and jiggle it to stop the crying.

"Wow, this is getting bad," he says.

"You have no fucking idea."

I decide it's a good day to wash windows. Not actually wash, but squirt them with Windex. I place The Baby in the carrier and put her in the heated porch in front of the TV.

Then I come back and Windex the kitchen windows while he's having his peanut butter sandwich.

"Do you have to use that ammonia stuff while I'm eating?"

"Yes. Yes, I fucking do."

He nods and continues chewing. When he's done, he leaves the plate on the table and makes for the basement stairs.

"Hey! The fucking plate goes in the dishwasher."

He comes back and puts it into the dishwasher.

"The knife, too," I say.

"Is there any coffee?"

"At Starbucks there is. Or you could try Dunkin Donuts. They both have fucking coffee."

"Right." He heads back down the basement stairs.

After I squirt every fucking window in the house, I decide to take a walk. I put The Baby into the stroller. My therapist is encouraging me to walk every day. It takes the stress out of your body, he said. I wondered about his choice of the word *body*. I feel under these particular circumstances that it wasn't the best choice. Couldn't he have said: *It lessens your stress.* Or something without the word *body*. It is bodies that got us into this mess in the first place. I don't need to be fucking reminded every moment. I'm thinking of switching therapists.

It's a damp day. April here in upstate New York can go either way. This year there's been a lot of dampness. Just what I don't need. The grass is still brownish and the trees are mostly without leaves. I need bright sunshine and some fucking warmth. But apparently I have no power over that. Or my marriage. Or my screaming baby. I am quite powerless. I only have power over the meals served in my house.

After my 5 mile walk (which I kind of doubt because I think my pedometer is off), I sit on the front steps of our house. A weak sun has come out. I park the stroller so The Baby will get some warmth on her face. I notice my neighbor has planted daffodils near the stone wall. I used to like daffodils a lot. Now they are just daffodils.

Lunch
by Gloria Garfunkel

I refuse to eat lunch at all. Some sort of chicken salad and greasy French fries.

"I don't eat fat," I say. "I'm allergic. It says it in my medical … um … chart. Also, I don't eat mayonnaise because it has … um … eggs … and I'm … um … vegan. Isn't that in my … um … record, too?"

The nurse, who looks like she has an eating disorder, insists I eat something.

"A salad with no dressing," I say.

"That's not a lunch," she says.

"Fine. Then a can of chocolate Ensure. And I want some black coffee."

"No coffee. You're not sleeping."

"Fine, then more ice water. Two pitchers this time. I've got to wash this … um … poison out so I can go home."

I've also got to fill myself up with something.

12.15pm
East Village, New York City, NY, USA

Kit and Dasha
by Kyle Hemmings

It is lunchtime. Kit is helping Dasha, her latest girlfriend, in the kitchen. The two are preparing a cucumber and radish salad with green onions. They are in Dasha's apartment overlooking a flower shop on East 3rd. The day has cleared up. The sun is shining through everything. Although it has grown warmer, a chill lingers.

"You don't have to help me," says Dasha, "it's not like I'm all thumbs."

"I don't want you to be lonely," says Kit.

"Speak for yourself, grunge-girl."

Dasha is twenty-one and attends art school. She is dressed in a check ribbon skirt and a tight white blouse. She and Kit met at a bar after Kit scored a trick with a college professor who reminded her of her stepdad. The crease in Dasha's nose always distracts Kit. She has drawn several charcoal nude portraits of Kit in the apartment, shades drawn, yet still enough light. Kit always claims that the drawn breasts are too large.

Dasha sometimes tells Kit after sex, "I love you, Kitty, but your legs are so thin and I wish you had bigger breasts."

And Kit replies, "And who made such an impression on your nose?"

Dasha sticks out her tongue. "It's called genetics."

"Science is amazing."

Leaning against the sink, Kit admires the way Dasha thinly slices the green onions and cucumbers. When Dasha is done, Kit pours a light sour cream with finely chopped dill over the onions and cucumber. She adds salt and pepper. The girls bring plates and the main salad into the dining room, which is no larger than Czarina's. Dasha pours them both a semi-sweet white wine, which Kit doesn't really like, but never complains.

While munching on their salads, the girls smile at each other or sometimes screw up their faces to make the other laugh.

Dasha pours for them a second glass of wine.

"Are you full, darling?" asks Dasha

"Yes, darlink," says Kit.

"I never say it as darlink, Beatle-juice girl."

The two reach over the table and hold hands.

"So tell me, Kitty Kat, I am just curious."

"About what?"

"The men, the ones you go out with. Do you enjoy it?"

"Sometimes. More often it's like ho-hum, I gotta do it."

"So you do enjoy it."

Kit pulls her hand away from Dasha and plays with her fork. She tries balancing the handle end on the edge of the table.

"You've had guys haven't you?"

"Da."

"So what's the big deal? They can't compete with you. Not for a million rubles."

Dasha smiles. Her teeth are white and perfect. "Look. Why don't you move in with me? It would be fun. And I'd have someone to wake up to. And someone to make salads for me when I'm not feeling very borscht. And you can get a job at the diner on East 5th and 3rd. They're hiring. Oh, say yes. I hate living alone."

The fork falls to the floor. Kit bends down in her chair and picks it up. Then rests her head on her hands, gives Dasha a soulful look, as if a diva posing for a CD cover.

"Later. Yeah. Maybe. Just not now. The woman that I'm living with, she's like my mom, you know?"

Dasha runs a hand through her cropped dirty blonde hair. "Yes, I know. Most of us have had mothers."

"I mean it's not like I don't want to. I do. But not now. Not this instant. She needs me."

"I see. And you need her."

"Something like that. There aren't too many kind people out there. This one took me in when I had nothing."

Dasha juts her chin forward. "You still have nothing."

"I have you."

"I was hoping, little bitch, that you'd say something like that."

Dasha lights a cigarette. Blows smoke past Kit's face.

Kit grabs the cigarette and throws it on the floor. "Don't you know smoking is bad for you, darlink?"

"You're not my babushka. If you are, we are morally decrepit. Dostoyevsky would disown us."

"I can't French you with that stale odor of cigarette smoke. Makes me feel weird."

"You are weird."

"We're both weird. Weird but good salad tossers."

Dasha pouts then offers a smile. Her dimples thrill Kit.

"I want to make love." She pounds a fist on the table.

"Right now?"

"Yes. This instant. Why wait until the sun goes down."

"But we just ate."

"And we drank wine and I'm feeling good. So what of it? You're not feeling good?"

Dasha shrugs. Kit tilts her head.

"I feel great," says Kit.

Holding hands, the girls head towards the sofa in the lightly furnished living room. Cheap reproductions adorn the walls. Copies of Van Gogh and Basquiat. Kit once pointed out that they were an odd combination. Dasha told her that it depends on one's perspective and that she never liked Warhol.

By the sofa, Kit removes her blouse. She's not wearing a bra. She pushes down her skirt, bends over to gather it from around her ankles. Standing over her, Dasha says, "What is that on your back?"

Kit tosses the skirt over Dasha's shoulder.

"They're called tattoos. They were done by the tattoo lady. She tattooed a menu to my back, so I'd never forget her. They're the names of all the dishes she taught me how to cook for her."

"Go, lie down on the sofa. Titties to the cushions."

Kit jumps on the sofa, drapes herself across the cushions.

Sitting beside her, Dasha fingers the letters and names. "How very cool," she says. "They're so glowing, slick. I want to lick them off."

"I have a very cool tattoo lady."

Dasha massages Kit's neck while poring over each tattooed item.

"I would like to order the sweet and sour cabbage dish, madam."

Kit's voice is low and muffled. "You're getting cold borscht, honey."

"Come live with me, darling," Dasha whispers in Kit's ear.

Kit smiles and turns her head to the sofa.

Lunch on the Run with Eggroll
by Walter Giersbach

The rain leaked dismally from a leaden sky as he left his publisher's office and stepped onto Canal St. He was being soaked by Heaven's tears of grief, the city's wounds, the world's suffering. God was crying over something.

He should have known a legit publisher didn't have offices on Canal, even if it was a single room. But Saltzman was the only one who'd accepted his manuscripts and boards. The only one who'd risked publishing a debut work. The reviews were golden, the sales lackluster.

Walking into the rain was less depressing than hearing Saltzman say, "Mikey, you pitched this Lucy Dingo theme and it didn't sell. I'm left with two-goddamn-thousand books. Come back with something new."

"I never got my royalty check for March."

Saltzman scribbled a check. Mike looked at the number in disbelief.

"Take it. Save me a stamp. Look, don't get mad. Just come up with some new ..."

Screw Saltzman. There had to be other publishers. At worst, he could work at his friend Ralph's graphics firm, lay out corporate brochures, design coffee mugs.

The royalty check was barely enough to buy food for a week, or he could splurge on a really memorable lunch.

Hong Fat's on Mott Street was just around the corner. Maybe hot tea, crispy rice soup and something stir-fried would take the chill away.

A finger tap-tapped his shoulder.

"Lunch? You're buying, of course, to show that you forgive me."

He whirled to face Calliope withdrawing her finger. She grinned, as though she were selling toothpaste. Her black hair ought to have resembled seaweed in this rain, but there was a natural wave. Super Sta-Hold hair lacquer, he decided. Acrylic that could also keep your head connected to your shoulders. Apparently she had also gone home to change the blue dress for black jeans and a black leather jacket. Tight jeans made her legs exceptionally long and curvy.

"Forgive you? You broke a plate in the sink." Good-looking women always thought they deserved a free ride. Be nice to them and they'd turn into praying mantises dancing over the bodies of genuine guys after biting off their heads.

"I know."

"From my mother's wedding set. It was irreplaceable."

"Nothing's irreplaceable, you nostalgic jerk." Her hands akimbo on her hips, she looked like a demented crossing guard.

"*People* are irreplaceable!"

"Well, that's debatable." She took his arm, a Virgil guiding him down the steps to Hong Fat's restaurant, although she might be escorting him to Dante's first circle of Hell. "People? My madam always finds me another date if one has a heart attack or his airplane crashes."

"You are so cynical!"

She smiled broadly. "Cynics are simply idealists with experience. I'll have a Sprite and some chop suey."

"There's no such thing as chop suey. That was invented by cooks stir-frying all the leftover crap in the kitchen for

133

the miners. Like *salsa puttanesca* Italian chefs whipped up when the hookers came in off the streets. Maybe that's more familiar to you."

"Sounds great. I'm just a glutton at heart."

He described the plates when their food arrived. "This is cold hacked chicken, these are steamed shrimp, beef *lo mein*, and this is stir-fried watercress. Start with the *shu-mai* dumpling."

She ignored him and began forking food into her mouth.

"Slow down! There's soup coming later."

Was she starving? Mike watched in fascination and she shoveled food into her mouth, slurping soda, and then turning to another platter for more. This woman was case history from Abnormal Psych 101. Maybe a runaway from Freaks Anonymous.

At last, she breathed a deep sigh, belched politely with a finger to her lips, and wiped her mouth, smearing the last of her lipstick on the white napkin. "That was marvelous. I have to learn this stuff."

Mike nodded. Without makeup, she looked as though she had taken off a mask after a Japanese Noh play. "Eating is the one vice you can do three times a day until you're too old to swallow."

Calliope leered in return. "If you're a woman, there's another vice ..."

"Does everything have to be about sex?" He tossed his chopsticks onto the plate. "Don't you have any deeper thoughts?"

"Well, yes, I've been thinking about you – *existential* thinking." She looked at him under lowered eyelids. "You wander down the mean streets of New York, but you're not really mean. You saved me and would have confronted those hoodlum kids, so I know you're not afraid and your soul is unblemished. That's nice. Rare. You're a common man, but you're unusual. Maybe a man of honor. Even rarer nowadays."

"What a nice speech. Thanks." He thought of their ping-pong conversations. "I mean that. Sincerely."

"So why are you so depressed? So," she shrugged, "filled with despondency under the surface?"

"That's a personal question."

"Yes, but since you saved my life I think it's fair to ask."

"I didn't save your mixed-up life. I saved your ass from the zombies and creeps that troll the streets after midnight. So you wouldn't get senselessly mugged and end up as roadkill on Hester Street."

"Maybe you did save my life. Maybe you should ask *me* some of those personal questions. Maybe I *was* going to kill myself last night, so now you're really and truly responsible for me."

"You're making me crazy! Can't you act normal without trying to take my life apart?"

"Actually, I was considering it. Killing myself. Some really bad guys are looking for me. I overheard a conversation when I was with a john. Remember the death of that mobster under the Brooklyn Bridge last week? Well, Johnny Four Fingers didn't accidentally run his BMW off the pier to go fishing."

"Jesus!" He exhaled.

"Apparently, he was double crossing someone for the Philadelphia mob. I just got a teensy bit drunk, wondering what to do."

Was it true or had she cribbed it from a TV show? "I think you ought to find a better class of john, someone with a positive career outlook."

This Calliope was a Typhoid Mary of destructive energy, someone who'd shed her problems like cat hair on everyone she came in contact with. Not content with being depressed, did she work to baste everyone she met with gooey unhappiness the way you'd slather a wine reduction over a piece of beef?

He threw down a bill, the same hundred she had tossed on his breakfast table. "This'll take care of the tab. I'm outta here."

He scraped his chair back. A *mélange* of anger, regret and disappointment stirred in him like a *bouillabaisse* of rotten ingredients.

"Don't you want to take the leftovers home in a doggy bag?" she scolded. "Hey, you forgot your fortune cookies. They're cheaper than therapy."

He wanted to leave her with one cutting insult, but a clap of thunder made the statement for him.

11.00am
Cherry Mountain, Texas, USA

Al's Kitchen
by Jonathan Levy

Hey, Cara, listen. I gotta tell you something. Now, you know we get some real characters coming in here every once in a while: people convinced we spit in their burgers, or swearing the antique something-or-other they just bought in Fredericksburg is worth a million, oh and of course all the locals who go on about how their own dear Texas should secede from the Union. But you've been working here only, what, ten months as of this past Monday? So you haven't met Howard Fletcher.

Howard was here this morning for breakfast – you may have seen me serving him. Friendly-looking old man. Wore a tweed jacket, got all this uncombed white hair sticking out the side of his head. Anyway, he'll likely be back for lunch around noon, noon-thirty. I'm telling you this now in case you interact with him, alright?

So let me tell you about Howard Fletcher. He ate here for the first time with his wife, Maggie, oh, about fifteen years ago. Just after he retired. They came in for breakfast, and Maggie liked the food so much, they came back for lunch that same day and then again for dinner. They've done that – eaten all three meals here – every year on this date, April 24th. It's Maggie's birthday. They drive up from Comfort, which is only 25 minutes south of here on 87. They spend the whole day in Fredericksburg – shopping, museums, maybe some live music – but still, she tells me every year that eating here is the best birthday gift. Real sweet lady, huh?

So I've always been their waiter. They're our most regular regulars, and I want to make it special for them. Not that, you know, if you served them, good looking gal like you and all ... Anyway, last year on this day was the last time I saw them both together.

Now Maggie was always a small, sprightly looking gal. Sure, I saw her age a bit, but it's like her hair turned more silver than gray. And she had these bright blue eyes, and the wrinkles around them were so subdued I could still see her face as a young girl.

Well, last year Howard shuffled in here in the morning arm in arm with a woman that made me do a double take. She was so tiny and shriveled I was surprised she could stand up, even with his help. Every step was an ordeal – she couldn't even step her heel past the toes on the other foot. And she was completely bald.

My first thought was that this woman was Howard's mother, who would've been at least 100 years old. I greeted them all smiles near the entrance, and then froze: there was no mistaking Maggie's blue eyes.

Howard and I helped her to the booth, and then they ate breakfast, same as always – two eggs, sunny side up, buttered toast, and a glass of OJ each. Maggie barely touched her plate, and they didn't even make it in for lunch or dinner. And that was the last time I saw Maggie Fletcher.

Anyway, Cara, here's the point. So Howard comes in this morning – 7:30, right when we open. He's alone, and you don't have to be a rocket scientist to know what that means. I greet him near the entrance, as always. I say, real quiet and serious, "How are you, Howard?"

"Oh fine!" he says, so chipper I flinch. "Can't wait for another special day at Al's Kitchen!"

I watch him as he walks to the nearest booth and swear he's muttering to himself.

Anyway, so I go over to him and say, "Start you off with an OJ?"

He says, "Two OJs, Al. No need to change things just because she's eighty."

I just stare at him and finally say, "No reason at all, Howard."

Now you're probably thinking what I was at that moment. He's gonna drink one down for his old lady, a sort of toast. So I say, "Get those right out for you." But he reaches out his arm just as I'm turning around and says, "And we'll get the usual, too."

"I'm sorry, what?"

"Two orders of the usual. You know, two eggs and some toast."

"Alright."

So I go back to make the eggs. Spread some butter on the grill. I turn around to glance back at Howard; he looks like he's talking to himself again, hand-gestures and all. I'm worried the poor guy's gone loony since Maggie passed. I crack four eggs over the grill, add a couple pieces of bread, pour two glasses of OJ, and head back out there with their, um, his drinks.

I set the OJs down in front of Howard and he says, "Thanks, Al," and then – I swear it, cross my heart – he pushes one glass across the table, picks up the other, and looks right across that table, right into the empty space opposite his seat, and says, "Happy birthday, dear. May you have many more."

Funny thing to say to a dead girl, you know? So I say, "Howard?" He looks up: "Hm?" And I just can't follow up, don't know what to say. He says, "Maggie, do you know what it is Al is trying to say?" Then he laughs.

"Are you alright, Al?" he says. Imagine that!

Finally I just say, "Get those eggs right out," and I leave.

As the eggs fry, I steal some more glances at Howard. He's having a conversation with his dead wife!

I don't know why, but the whole thing just … I smash the yolks with a spatula, press them so they ooze yellow all over the grill. Then I butcher them, turn them into a giant scramble of hardened yellow and white and mucus-y looking stuff. Meanwhile, I've forgotten all about the bread, which is burned on the bottom. I flip them over and slap some butter onto the burnt side, then smash the goddamn butter and the bread with it.

I'm sorry, Cara, I shouldn't … I … Where was I?

Oh, yeah, so I bring the food out, say to Howard, "Hey, sorry, hope you don't mind them scrambled."

He says, "Maggie, is scrambled alright with you?" In the silence my head bounces between Howard and the empty space like I'm at a tennis match, till he nods and tells me, "That's fine."

I say, "Enjoy the eggs, Howard." I don't know what came over me, Cara, but then I say, "You, too, Maggie." As if she's right there!

Her eggs don't get eaten of course, but I can't help but laugh later on when Howard asks me to box them up to go.

Anyway. Cara. One more thing. It's that … I just feel so damn bad for the guy, you know? Here he is, been with the love of his life for about sixty years, and now he's all alone. I guess this is how he copes, but … dammit, it's not real! He talks to her, but no one talks back; reaches out to touch her, but there's nothing there. Not like, you know, this wall. This wall is right here and it's real and look, I can touch it and my hand doesn't go through it. This picture of Willie Nelson is real; I can see the image. And you, you're standing right here, so close I can touch you, and you're real. Everything about you: your hair and your eyes, all real; your body, your

140

legs, all real. Your lips ... they're real. You. You're standing right here and you're real and I am completely and madly in love with you, Cara. And there's nothing more real than that.

Two Plus One for Tea
by Gill Hoffs

He's pleasantly surprised by Alan's flat. Bright yellow walls, colourful rugs, and barely a whiff from the Chinese takeaway below. As the boy shows him to the living room-cum-kitchen and points out the bathroom door a tabby of monstrous proportions jumps off the sofa with an audible *thump* then slinks round Alan's ankles and yowls. The boy picks it up and the cat immediately clambers onto his shoulders, peeping at the visitor with milky orange eyes.

"This is Clarice. Clarice, this is ... what's your name?"

"Bert. Bert Humphries."

He's never been introduced to a cat before.

"Clarice, Bert. Bert, Clarice."

"How do." He hopes he's not expected to shake her paw or owt daft like that.

"Clarice is getting on a bit and her eyes are going but so long as you don't surprise her she's fine."

"What happens if I surprise her? By accident, like?"

The boy pulls the sleeve of his t-shirt back from his wrist, showing tattoos marred by the parallel red furrows of a cat scratch. "She doesn't mean any harm by it, she's dead soft really, but if she gets a fright she's all claws and teeth."

"I'll bear that in mind." And stay the hell away from her if she's going to do something like that, he thinks.

"Well, I need to get on with dinner so make yourself at home. The TV goes on with the green button on the remote and you're welcome to watch what you like, or stick on a DVD," he points to several stacks by the wall, "read the paper or come and help me, if none of that appeals." He bends at the waist, letting the cat walk down his back then jump from his rear end to the couch. Straightening up, he smiles before walking behind the breakfast bar into the adjoining kitchen area.

Hoping the boy isn't planning on cooking fish (ugh, mackerel), he wanders across to the window. A child waves to him from a double decker bus but is gone before he gets his hand up to wave back. From here he can see across to the spire of the church where Marie's buried. There's a golden weathercock at its tip and a rare moment of sun makes it gleam. Then the cat jumps on the windowsill, neatly avoiding the pots of cacti and swats at the crystal stars dangling from the catch, so he turns away.

"What you cooking, lad?"

He can see a mound of vegetables by a chopping board, like in an advert for soup, and the boy's rummaging about in a cupboard near the sink.

"Bean pie." His voice is muffled 'til he stands up with a colander. "My mum's coming over for tea so I'm making something hearty. She's on her own so she doesn't cook much, and it's nice to have an excuse to make something proper. Expand my culinary horizons and so on."

The boy starts rinsing peppers under the tap and since he doesn't fancy getting shredded by Clarice, he walks into the kitchen area to help. The breakfast bar is covered in bowls of fruit, piles of magazines, bags of onions, some purple, some brown, a box of mushrooms, and a proper leek like his dad grew with all the greenery intact.

"Where'd you find this beauty? Not seen one like that in years. Don't know why the supermarkets trim them down so. Nowt on 'em usually and the green's the best bit."

"My mum's got an allotment by the canal, she brings me all sorts for here and the caff."

He's intrigued by the peppers and the presence of the leek, he's never heard of bean pie and can only visualise a lump of pastry covering a dish of baked beans.

"What you doing with them peppers?"

The boy finishes drying them on a cloth and plonks them down next to the chopping board. "I chop them fine with an onion and some leek – you could get on with the mushrooms while I do these, if you want to help – and fry them a little with some butter, just to soften them. Then I add some beans, once I've rinsed them, and red lentils and pepper. A good squirt of garlic paste, some tinned tomatoes, and gravy powder and it's done."

He scrapes some muck off the mushrooms and starts chopping with what Marie would've called a fruit knife that he finds in the block. "Do you want the stalks left on 'em?"

The boy is pushing the stalk into a yellow pepper with his thumbs.

"Sure, so long as they're chopped fine. Thanks."

He watches while the boy then sticks his thumbs into the hole left by the stalk and pulls the pepper in two, emptying the stalk and clump of seeds onto a dirty plate. He does the same trick with the other peppers then plucks a carving knife from the block and starts to dice them. When he gets close to his fingertips Bert can't look and returns his focus to the mushrooms. When they're done, he leaves them on the board and washes the leek. The boy has a good-sized pile of diced peppers now and from the smell of it has started on the onions.

"Do you want the whole leek doing?"

"Please, though I'll only use maybe half of it. The rest can go for stew later."

Soon the frying pan is spitting and the aroma is making his mouth water so much that he has to swallow before he speaks. "The leek's done, what now?"

144

The boy's stirring but pauses to turn and grab a handful of the greens, dropping them in the pan with the rest of the veg. The kitchen's just the right size for two to work in, with everything in comfortable reach. The kind of kitchen he'd find manageable. "Could you take the lids off the tins and rinse the beans in the colander please? Chuck them in together, it's all getting mixed anyhow."

Cannellini beans. Were they named after an opera singer or was that just Marie's teasing? He doesn't like to ask. In they go with the kidney beans and black eyed peas, quick rinse, then the boy takes it off him and empties the contents into the pan.

"Do you want me to roll out the pastry?"

"It's not that kind of pie. If you look in the fridge there's a bowl of grated cheese and a dish of mashed potato. Could you get them both out and stick the potato in the microwave on medium for a couple of minutes?"

There's food on every shelf, all sorts of sauces and leftovers and puddings and cheeses. You can barely see to the back of it. He thinks of his own fridge with its packet of ham slices and rind of cheese and resolves to stock up next time he's in the supermarket. He can afford to now. With the potato warming and the cheese out, the boy stops stirring the contents of the frying pan and bends to light the oven.

"What now?"

"Now I'll use last night's mash for a topping, only I'll add garlic paste and this extra mature cheddar then sprinkle it with more cheese aaaaand ..." he reaches behind a packet of muesli, "the magic ingredient, crumbled crisps. Makes it chewy and works better than crumbs, or so I like to think. If you put the kettle on you could make us a brew while I get on with this."

The kettle's purple which fits with the rainbow effect of the rest of the flat. As the boy tips the contents of the frying pan into a long terracotta dish, Bert sources some teabags in a jar shaped like a pink toad and takes the milk from the fridge. He's intrigued by the boy's finicking with the mashed potato, dithering about with a butter knife and spreading fingerlengths of it against the edge of the dish, then realises this is perhaps where he's been going wrong with his shepherd's pie which always ends up with a dollop in the middle and the mince mixed into it in an unappetising grey-brown mush.

As the boy lifts the dish into the oven a buzzer goes off somewhere near the front door. According to his watch it's only half six.

"Could you go let my mum in while I clean up a bit? The door release is beside an internal phone, looks like a light switch. I've two minutes to sort the place before I get a telling off."

She's older than he expected, closer to his age than his son's, and shares the boy's smiley nature.

"How do, I'm Joan. Are you not too warm in that coat?"

And he realises that he is. And he's hungry, and happy, and attracted to her.

Eight o'clock is coming far too soon.

Kapustnica
by Andrew Stancek

David looks up and sees an angel, blonde curls, dimpled cheeks, touching his forehead. He tries to lift his head. He tries to speak. She touches a finger to his lips and whispers, "Sleep."

In his fevered dream he's running from a fire which transforms into a rapacious dragon, and David cannot pull that sword out of its scabbard. As the sharp teeth clamp on his arm, he wakes and finds he hasn't metamorphed but is in a hospital bed, body throbbing and disoriented. Tubes snake out of his arm. A male nurse plunges a needle into his thigh and David coughs but cannot move his strapped torso. He drifts off.

"Totally against hospital policy and against medical advice," the shrill voice is yelling. "Doctor Zajko said another day's observation and tests are needed. Barging in like this is an outrage, and you have no right ..." David feels straps released, blankets removed. He opens his eyes and knows he is still in a dream: Taia is touching him and grinning. Ferko is throwing clothes onto the hospital bed, shooing off the angry buzz.

"Let's get a move on here, old-timer, before we change our minds and call off the rescue. You only get to scare your friends once a day. I've brought you back to life, brought you The Beloved and now it's time to fly this coop and eat.

I'm starving and I know you are, too." David's head is spinning but with the help of Taia scrunches arms into sleeves, has a sweater pulled over his head, stumbles up, is half-carried into an elevator and is in a downpour again. Ferko laughs but David only squints at Taia, two Taias, three Taias; he's about to fall. It's her perfume, his eyes might be deceiving him but his nose is not, is he touching her or is she a vision? He needs to pinch, or even better bite her, but both his arms are held as he sways.

"You can thank me for saving your life later," Ferko yells into the downpour. "While you were busy walking into traffic and getting hospitalized, I found her. And look, she's not about to push you off the new Danube Bridge. We have to get you plumped up. No more of this 'I can't eat a bite'. Down this road. The best *kapustnica* in all of Bratislava. Forest mushrooms, home-made sausage, oak-barrel wine sauerkraut." He drops David's arm. David stands on his own feet, head woozy but he's alive. She came back. He tries to touch her but she moves off. Her smile is forced. Ferko pushes the door of the restaurant open, yells, "Three servings of *kapustnica*. That's for me. I don't know what my friends will have." Taia giggles, looks at David but when he grins, she looks away and sits hard on the wooden bench. David collapses next to her and nuzzles his head in her shoulder. Her hair. He'll faint. The rooster in his head is crowing. The raven is swooping around the restaurant. David's stomach rumbles, screams. Maybe he can eat after all.

8.12pm
Cyclades Islands, Greece

Hundreds
by Lyn Fowler

The sun is just setting when we hear the putt-putt of Sestos' blue and yellow wooden boat. He pulls alongside our boat and collects John (now known as Yiannis on this trip). They motor out into the little bay only 100 metres away. We can see their shadowy figures bobbing with the boat. The light is receding now but they work quickly and quietly pulling in the net. Then they are heading back to our boat. Fresh from the net Sestos brings a bucket of slippery silver fish onto our boat and feeds them through the open porthole. The two of us in the galley catch the fish still flapping alive.

"There's hundreds," I cry out. Not daunted, I pat them dry with paper towel. Then we form an assembly line, quickly dusting the whole fish in plain flour with salt and pepper and then without overcrowding the pan, frying them in batches in shallow olive oil. The cooking is only 15 seconds on each side turning once but there are so many fish. The dented aluminium pan on the gas cooker is cooking them beautifully golden. I am worried that the galley and cabins will be full of smoke any minute. The oil must be hot enough to cook the fish quickly and crisply. Kostas from above keeps a concerned eye on the production in the galley. Everyone has a job to do. I keep going with my skilful hand on the spatula. I think that he has not seen so many people in the galley before.

"Where's the wine?" I turn to see Yiannis lifting a cord from the side of the boat.

"Voila, nicely chilled I'd say. We do not see corks much these days at home. I miss the sound of the cork coming out of the bottle."

"Yes, but what happens when you forget the corkscrew. You should always keep one in your car or your yacht in this case."

Yiannis extracts the cork easily and he pours the wine into glasses. "Yamas," we chorus and clink our glasses together.

We have a mountain of fish to feed six people. The only accompaniment needed is Sestos' ripe tomatoes and a squeeze of juicy lemon that I roughly cut into quarters. I had cooked some pasta earlier feeling not optimistic about the fish catch. We will use the pasta another time. I need more faith; there is a bounty out there in the water.

Sestos says that the fish are so sweet because they feed off the rocks around the islands where it is brimming with small food and plankton.

Yiannis drops down the steps and lifts up the platter of cooked marida from the galley. He places the platter on an upturned box so we can all be close to the food. We are all eating with our fingers de rigueur. The fish are crisp and tender. The tomatoes are just as sweet as the ones at our earlier picnic on Sestos' island. The squeeze of lemon adds a juicy tang. No one is looking around for other sauces or flavours. The meal is complete.

I sip my wine from a glass tonight. It is red wine and with a slight chill from the earlier dangling in the Aegean. The breeze has dropped and the water is still. Even our boisterous chatter has quietened. We are mellow, well fed and reflective.

We wave goodnight to Sestos. We send him home with a bottle of wine with much appreciation. Kostas shines a large torch to light the way back to the jetty as he putters off home.

We lie back on the deck and look up at a trillion stars. I am dozing under the heavens. Before tonight, I had not eaten fish from the sea to the table in under an hour.

Two and a Leaner
by Paul Beckman

Martin was running late because his boss called to wish him a happy birthday this fine April day and then took his time thanking him for getting a report out on time. Carrying a bag from the market he ran up the stairs to his apartment, key in hand, and let himself in, tossing his jacket as he made his way to the refrigerator where he pulled out the mayo, pickles, fried peppers, hot sauce, olives and lettuce.

He opened his bag and took out a twelve inch grinder roll, sliced it in half and slathered both sides with mayo and stone ground mustard while all the time sneaking peeks out the kitchen window over the sink to the apartment across the way. The kitchen was still dark so Betty Ann hadn't arrived home for lunch yet and he calmed a bit. Martin sliced the olives and sprinkled them on both sides of the roll and then added big slices of fried peppers. He then reached inside his bag from the market and took out a container of egg salad which he spread also on both sides and then added more mayo. He liberally poured the hot sauce and then layered one side with bread and butter pickles and saw the light come on in Betty Ann's kitchen.

He turned off the ceiling light, folded the halves of the sandwich over and positioned his camera with its zoom lens and tripod in the space between the sink and the window and closed the curtains so only the lens protruded.

Betty Ann came home every day for lunch and was a creature of habit. Not wanting to spill anything on her clothes she stripped down to her bra and panties, that is, when she wore underwear which was only some of the time. She poured herself a glass of red wine, took a sip and then walked to the refrigerator and took out her sandwich fixings. It was always the same, a croissant, egg salad and a tall glass dish of Jello along with a can of whipped cream. Eating egg salad also made Martin feel as if they were dining together.

Martin took his sandwich, too big for one hand, in both hands, hefted it, leaned over the sink and took a big bite never taking his eyes off Betty Ann. This is the kind of sandwich his father called "two and a leaner": two hands to hold it and lean over the sink so as not to get yelled at by Martin's mother for spilling food on the floor.

The mayo ran down his chin but he'd have to put down the sandwich to wipe it so he ignored it and took another bite. If he wasn't leaning over the sink the sandwich would be leaking everywhere it shouldn't.

Betty Ann looked out the window across at her neighbor's apartment as she chewed her egg salad sandwich. She put the sandwich down and picked up her binoculars and trained them on the apartment next door to Martin's.

Betty Ann took another sip of wine and a few drops dribbled onto her breast and she smiled and rubbed it into her nipple and then licked her finger. Martin gobbled two more bites and wished she would step back from the sink so he could see her altogether and at that moment she turned and walked to the counter for a napkin. Excited at seeing her dimpled ass and her trimmed bush, he stopped eating and watched Betty Ann wipe her mouth and then her breast. She picked up her sandwich and took a big bite and some egg salad dribbled out of the corner of her lips. Daintily she pushed it back into her mouth and sucked on her finger. *This is the best April 24th ever,* Martin thought out loud.

Putting down the last of the sandwich, Betty Ann lifted the dish of Jello and spooned a bit into her mouth and then shook the can of whipped cream and covered the Jello. Martin held his sandwich and stared as Betty Ann filled a large spoon with whipped cream covered Jello and sucked it off the spoon. She then shook the can of whipped cream again and squirted a large spurt directly into her mouth – head tilted back. Martin almost bit off a finger with the size of the bite he took. He chewed and the more he chewed the more mayo dribbled out as he watched Betty Ann swish the whipped cream in her mouth and leak out as she smiled, lips slightly open. She left the whipped cream in lines dripping down to her chest and picked up her binoculars and seemed to be looking directly at Martin's window. Martin dropped his sandwich remains in the sink and rubbed the mayo over his mouth and chin then sucked it off his fingers, one by one.

Betty Ann smiled and took another spoon of Jello while Martin scooped a handful of mayo and headed for his bedroom.

12.30pm
Forth Worth, Texas, USA

In Between a Sandwich
by Tom Fegan

Lunch for me was at Subway Joe's. A national chain that promotes healthy eating through submarine sandwiches. They had other varieties for those not on a diet. I cheated some but only a little at this eatery. I ordered my usual turkey breast foot long on Italian bread with tomatoes, spinach, black olives and green peppers. My cheat was Swiss cheese. Ranch dressing covered the goods. I took the sandwich and unsweetened tea to a vacant table and slid into a seat. A quick blessing and thus began my attack. It was a needed break. The D.A. had not responded to my report about the murder of the tomboy Gerry Day.

I munched and mulled on the evidence acquired against Ben Tomlinson, Gerry's neighbor. I had interviewed him in his prison cell. He declined both being interrogated with a lie detector as well as having blood drawn. Tomlinson did allow me to swab the inside of his mouth. Before I left he bounded to his feet, "I want a deal."

I turned, "You want to confess?"

Tomlinson dropped on his bunk and shook his head. He waved me out of his cell. I grimly departed. His confession would clinch the case with the binding evidence I had. I may have pushed him too hard.

"I don't know if I can convict with what you have Jonson," District Attorney Earle Bowles had observed. "The blood splatter inside the girl's car matched her DNA. Tomlinson's saliva was a match to the cigarette butt. The violence of the crimes committed were close and similarly intense. You reported his actions after the interview, but there were no other witnesses to verify it. You can't call it a near confession. His lawyer will feed it to you."

"Let a jury decide," I'd retorted and stormed out of his office. I paused from eating my submarine sandwich and listened to the murmur of other customers speak of their income taxes. They were oblivious to the crime surrounding them in the streets. I envied them.

A man in a dark business suit straightened his glasses and proudly showed a woman across from him photos of his children. "My tax deductions," he mused. I wasn't a parent. I couldn't relate but grimly focused on the Day family and their loss. Gerry loved mechanics and kept her vehicle in pristine condition. A true individual who was happier with tools than a manicure. Her parents spoke of her smile as she worked tirelessly on her car. That car was now evidence.

I picked up my cell phone. It was the D.A.'s office. Bowles wanted to see me. I finished the sandwich and discarded my trash on the way out. I was ready for an answer of any kind.

12.35pm
Cherry Mountain, Texas, USA

Slice of Life
by Jonathan Levy

Welcome back, San Antonio. I am Raymond Rothstein, and you are listening to 90.5 FM, KSAT radio. It is now 12:30 on a Friday, which means it's time for another 'Slice of Life', a short program in which I report live from a restaurant in a rural area outside San Antonio and strike up a conversation with a customer. Together, we learn about that person – his or her past, present, perspective on life and the people in it – and perhaps in the process, we learn something about ourselves, too. Right now, I sit in a red vinyl booth by the window of Al's Kitchen, a small diner in the town of Cherry Mountain, just northwest of Fredericksburg. Joining me across the table is Howard Fletcher. Why don't you tell our listeners a little about yourself, Howard?

"Well, I'm 83 years old. I grew up in the nearby town of Comfort, Texas, where I've lived most of my life. I had never been outside of Comfort until I left home to attend Texas State University in San Marcos. But I never finished college because I joined the Army. It wasn't until I came back from Korea in 1953 that I met Maggie Barnes, the prettiest girl I'd ever seen ... No, I mean it. We married in 1955."

I noticed the wedding band. You're still married now, I take it?

"Of course. In fact, Maggie is –"

"Welcome to Al's Kitchen. I'm Al, as in Al's Kitchen. Two unsweetened iced teas?"

Actually, I don't want anything to –

"You know us well, Al."

"Alright. Iced teas coming up."

Uh … Howard, how often do you eat here?

"First time was 17 years ago today. Something is bothering Al. He's usually much happier."

Seventeen years, wow. And what brings you here now?

"Well, we come every year for breakfast, lunch, and dinner on this day. It's Maggie's birthday. And today is extra special – we're celebrating her 80th."

We? I didn't know she would be joining you. I hope she'll speak to our listeners as well when she gets here.

"Actually, she's –"

"Two *un*sweetened iced – Oh no! I'm so sorry, Howard. Did I spill any on you? You look fine, phew! Hi, Howard, how are you? Who's your friend? Oh my gosh, I'm sorry, I haven't even – I'm Cara, I work here, of course. What's that thing in your hand for?"

I'm interviewing Howard for a radio program.

"You work for the radio? That's great! Sometimes I listen to those shows where people call in for advice about stuff. Do you work on a show like that? You know, like relationship advice? Listen. Let me tell you a secret. This morning, Al, the guy who owns the place? He told me he was in love with me. What should I do? I mean, I like him and all – he's a nice guy. But he's also my boss, you know?"

I'm sorry, I don't –

"Shoot, here he comes. See ya!"

"Two veggie burgers, Howard?"

"Yes indeed."

"Alright. Coming up."

Howard, when will Maggie be here?

"Hmm? She's right here."

I'm sorry – Where?

"Sitting right next to you."

Your wife is ... where I'm pointing?

"Yes, of course."

Howard, will you excuse me? I need to step outside. I'll be right ... Thank you for listening to this live broadcast of 'Slice of Life' from Al's Kitchen in Cherry Mountain, Texas. I know you cannot see what I see here, so I will do my best to describe it. Moments ago, you all heard Howard tell me that his wife, Maggie, sat right next to me. Now, I assure you, there was no one there – only empty space. Was Howard ever married at all? Is he hallucinating? And if so, why? Let's see if we can figure ... Excuse me, Cara? Do you know Howard Fletcher's wife, Maggie?

"Oh. Well, yes, I ... just met her this morning. They were here for breakfast."

You saw her here?

"Well, I didn't *see* Maggie. I mean she wasn't *here* here. It's just ... I'm sorry, Al told me she died of cancer over the last year and he felt bad because they'd spent their whole lives together and now Howard thinks he sees her then Al told me he was in love with me and I don't know what to do about it."

I ... um ... Excuse me, it looks like Howard is talking to his wife right now ... Hello, Howard, thank you for waiting. You know, I don't believe I've formally met your wife yet. It's nice to meet you, Maggie.

"Howard?"

"Hi, Cara."

"How long have you and Maggie been married?"

"It'll be 60 years in June."

Howard, do you ever wonder ... um ...

"Yes?"

It's just … don't you … I'm sorry, Howard, hold on one moment. Dear listeners, it looks like love is contagious here in Al's Kitchen. Our waitress, Cara, has made up her mind, and right now she and Al stand facing each other by the counter, holding hands and laughing.

"Were you asking me something, Raymond?"

Yes … no! I … Tell us about your wife, Howard.

"Maggie? Well, what can I say? She's the love of my life. Maggie is the kind of person who will make you smile just by looking at you. I knew it from the first moment I saw her. In fact, let me tell you about the day we met …"

After-Service Luncheon
by AR Neal

Bud smacked Justin in the back of his head as he sank his ample butt into the last free chair in the living room. "How you gonna sit up in my sister's house?"

"Don't you mean 'my lodge brother's house'?" Justin shot back.

"Justin Spirts, don't you start with me." Bud shook his hand in the other man's face. "How you gonna sit up in here and talk about my nephew like that? Jimmy's got a few issues, but you got no right!"

Justin snorted. "Jimmy's got more than issues. He's out there on that stuff and you know it. That's why he wasn't at his daddy's funeral."

"He was, too. I saw him in the back of the church," Odessa said. "Nancy said he walked to the cemetery from there." She winked at Justin. "And the boy *does* have issues."

Bud hefted his frame from the chair and stood up. "Odessa, you would take Spirts' side anyway."

They stopped talking as Nancy walked into the room. "What are y'all on about over here?"

"Bud was messin' with Justin about —"

"Nothin'," Bud interrupted. "We was just jaw-jackin'." He knew Nancy would be angry if Odessa shared that they

161

had been talking about Jimmy and his habits. "You know how Justin and the rest of those stuffy lodge boys are. I was tryin' to get him to show me the handshake."

"Uh-hm," Nancy looked him up and down. She suspected they had been talking about her oldest son but let it go; it was the wrong day for family to be at odds. She smiled. "How about James?" she said. "He was telling me how well he's doing these days."

"What's he doing?" Odessa asked. She was always ready for something to gossip about.

"He's working at one of those can and bottle recycle places. Some kinda manager or something."

"Managin' to sell cans and bottles to get them drugs, more like," Justin snickered, balancing a forkful of potato salad. Bud elbowed Justin's hand and the salad plopped on the edge of the plate.

Nancy frowned at them. "From the sounds of things, he's doing better. You know that recession hit young men like him awful hard."

"That only happened to people who were actually working, Ma," Jamal added, slipping past her with a plate full of cookies, cake slices, and a large piece of sweet potato pie. She swatted at him and he dodged her hand. "Where is he anyway? I didn't even get to talk with him."

"Don't you speak about your brother that way, young man. Anyway, I made him a plate since he had to go. Can you believe they have him scheduled to work this afternoon?" She crossed her arms tightly and hugged her elbows. "On the day of his daddy's funeral and they wouldn't let him off. He had to be there," she leaned around Jamal to look at the mantel clock, "at 3.00 so I gave him car fare."

Sighs of disgust filled the room. Nancy looked at them in surprise. "What's wrong with all of you?"

"Ma, Jimmy didn't need car fare," Jamal answered.

162

"He's not a manager. He hustled you."

Nancy blinked. "Don't talk that way about James. Don't let me hear *any* of you talking that way. Daddy wouldn't approve." She frowned, turned, marched into the dining room, and smiled at the Reverend and William, who were deep in discussion.

Odessa shoved a last spoonful of the Ambrosia into her mouth. She swallowed, looked toward Nancy in the next room and whispered, "She might not think so but Calvin knew all about James. And no, he didn't approve." She looked at Bud and Justin and gave them both a dagger-eyed stare. "You two know how she is about that boy. Now leave it alone. Today isn't about James, anyway." She turned toward Jamal, who was sitting in the corner, and asked, "Jamal, is that your mamma's lemon cake you got there? I gotta get me some of that before it's gone!" She licked her fork, and clutching her plate, stood up, and left in search of another of her favorite desserts.

Nancy shook her head, wanting to block her son's words about Jamal from her mind as she joined William and the Reverend as they stood near the punch bowl. William wiped the last of his chocolate cake from the corners of his mouth, and stood up straight.

"Nancy, how are you?" William asked. "I haven't seen you sit still since everyone arrived back here from the cemetery. Have you eaten?"

She waved him off. "I can't eat a bite just now, but I'm all right. I hope you're both enjoying the food."

Reverend Jones, Nancy's sister Stella's husband, shook his head. "Of course. You know I did." He leaned in. "When you gonna teach your sister to cook like this?"

Nancy tapped him lightly on the arm. "Stella's gonna get you for making fun of her cooking!"

"Ma. I need to talk to you." Jamal stood by her side, touching her elbow.

163

"Not now, Jamal."

"It's important."

She turned, saw the frown on his face, then looked past him and saw a police officer stood in the front doorway.

"It's about Jimmy, Ma."

Jamal took Nancy by the arm and guided her through the groups of family and friends, all quietly pushing food around their half-eaten plates.

"Mrs. Washington, I am so sorry to disturb you but there's been an incident involving your son, James. I'm going to need you to come with me to the hospital."

Nancy shrugged Jamal's hand away and replied, "Officer, I don't know if you are aware but we are celebrating my husband's home-going today. Now why don't you just rest yourself there – Bud, move over so the officer can sit down – and let me make you a plate. There's plenty as you can see. I know James is fine. I gave him car fare to get to work just about a half-hour ago, so what is this all about?"

The officer touched the edge of his cap. "Thank you, ma'am but no. I can't give you any additional information here and need you to come with me to the hospital. Your other son – Jamal? – said he would drive you."

Nancy wiped her palms down the front of her apron and reaching around, untied the knot at the back.

"Cora-Lynn," Nancy said, "get my purse from upstairs, would you? Stella, I didn't say thank you when I was in the dining room so please give my thanks to your husband for the message today. I know Daddy would have been very happy. Bud, you leave Justin alone while I'm gone and Justin, be sure to tell the brothers how much I appreciate all they did. I'll bring something nice around to the lodge next week as snacks for the meeting. And Odessa, make sure everybody gets some of this food to take home, especially the Reverend and William. And make sure Bertram doesn't take all of the macaroni salad — tell him to leave some for other folks."

Nancy glanced in the mirror next to the door and patted down a stray hair.

"I want that kitchen empty when I get back," she continued. "But save some of those oxtails. I want to freeze them for James because they're his favorite."

As Nancy and Jamal followed the officer down the porch steps, Stella called out, "Should I make you a plate too, Nancy?"

"No, that's all right, Stella," Nancy replied. "This is Daddy's day. I'll find something when we get back." Nancy turned to the officer. "We're going to the hospital?"

He nodded.

"Well," she paused by her potted flowers next to the bottom step and grabbed a handful of daffodils and pansies. "If James has been hurt or something, I'm sure some flowers will brighten up his room. Don't you think, Jamal?"

Jamal glanced at the officer, who shook his head slightly. "Sure, Ma. I'm sure that will be fine."

"Of course it will." Nancy gave Jamal and the officer a shaky smile as they walked toward the curb where Jamal's rental car was parked. Turning to Jamal as he opened the car door, Nancy asked, "Did I tell you how much Daddy loved daffodils?"

"Yes, Ma," Jamal said, "you sure did."

2.30pm
Acton, Massachusetts, USA

Fabric
by Michael Webb

It is the peak of the day, 2.30pm, finally time for the long delayed feasting, when everyone who is coming is here, and the house is as full as it is going to be. The smells fill the house, every breath redolent with the stink of flesh and carbohydrates and sauces. It is hot, not intolerably so, but stuffy, too many people in too small a space, and I can feel tiny areas of sweat drying as I move, the back of each knee and the small of my back damp where the fabric of my clothes presses too tightly. There is noise, children's voices chattering, male voices talking football, the thump of the video gamers coming up from downstairs, my mother talking animatedly to my aunt and my grandmother, some intricate piece of office politics that, like a traffic story, is interesting only to the teller.

I straighten all the way up, sucking my belly in as I rise, sliding my stockinged feet into my shoes. It feels heady, almost dizzy, to suddenly rise after being on the floor. I had been lying there, letting my cousin Chandler run his toy train over my legs and feet, the tiny wheels making even, smooth lines on my tights. His mother would occasionally glance at him with alarm, but I didn't mind. I knew that the tiny wooden wheels might snag and rip the thin fabric, but I had more pairs, and it was vaguely pleasant, the parallel pressures across my skin. Chandler had scrambled off, looking for his mother, his train forgotten on the floor. I crouch to pick up the toy, my head swimming again when I straighten. I put it onto a table behind me, hopefully within his line of sight.

It is distressingly easy to get lost in a crowd like this, and I had divined in the last few years the keys to making people think you had eaten when you hadn't. Always make sure you are seen with food, and be sure to be around people who are eating. I feel my heart pound inside my chest when I take a deep breath, and I endure a spasm of nauseous hunger in my gut. I wall it off, misusing my therapist's favorite trick, pushing the hunger into a steel gray safe and spinning the dial, closing my eyes for a moment until the feeling passes. Control, I think, feeling an icy dark thrill as I deny myself again. This, I control. This.

I watch my aunt, her body still thick with baby weight, making him a plate, small arrangements of white and green and red and orange and brown. I know he won't eat it, and I know she has to try anyhow, and I try to remember what it felt like, having someone else make all the decisions and trusting that they mean you no harm, and I want to weep with the relief of how that must be, and then I step forward into the space behind her, selecting food that I will carefully pretend to eat. I picture my body as forged steel, hard, carved and cold and inviolate.

Snack
by Gloria Garfunkel

A nurse brings me some red jello.

"Here is something you can eat," she says. "It's full of protein."

"I'm vegan and jello is full of … um … gelatin. It comes from … um … boiled pig skins and … um … bones. And I'm allergic to … um … food coloring. Don't they put these things in my … um … chart? Also, I don't eat sugar. Allergic too."

Jello is pure poison. It's not even food.

"It says here you make many excuses not to eat."

"They're not excuses. They're reasons."

Birthday Dinner
by Paul Beckman

At three forty-five Martin hung up the phone and at four on the dot Martin's kitchen counter was clear and he left home and quick-stepped to his car and drove off to Hanami, his favorite Japanese restaurant. His take-out was ready and he handed his credit card to the cashier, who saw him every Friday. Knowing he was in a hurry she swiped it and handed the receipt for his signature. Today he tipped generously. After all, this was his birthday dinner.

Yesterday he had brought them an oval platter and asked to have his meal set on it. He ordered extra ginger and wasabi but no salad or miso soup. He deserved a nice cold bottle of sake for this special occasion.

He drove to the temperature controlled storage unit he rented and set up his dinner on a series of cardboard boxes. His end unit on the second floor had a window.

Martin arranged the tripod and binoculars to look into the gym and shower room in the next building.

He checked over his maki rolls: salmon avocado with cucumber, rainbow roll, out-of-control roll with shrimp, breaded and fried, scallions and jalapeños, and a triple delight, lobster, salmon and redfish wrapped in thinly sliced cucumber and rolled in salmon roe. And one extra special birthday piece. He opened the sake, poured some into his porcelain sake cup and set them both down neatly.

He took out the chopsticks from the paper holder, poured the soy sauce into the small rectangular sauce holder that came with the set and dished the wasabi and ginger into their own saucers. He added wasabi to the soy sauce, mixed them together with a single chopstick, and then with the other chopstick added a bit of wasabi onto each piece of roll. After that he draped each piece with a ginger slice. As he did that he realized that he was making a kind of Japanese sandwich.

He opened the window a couple of inches so as to hear the music from the class. Martin then sat in his swivel chair, adjusted the field glasses and turned on the nightlight, shining a shard of light onto his meal. He pulled a string and turned off his overhead light and sat in the darkness thinking thoughts of sushi and women and toasted himself a happy birthday with a few sips of sake.

At five thirty the teacher came in and was soon followed by four other women and then a fifth, Marci, the one he was waiting for, straggled in. Betty Ann and Mandy were all ready there and waiting. This was a free form dance class. He watched as the women shed their street clothes in the locker room and left for the adjacent gym to work out in their skimpy shorts and tops that left their bellies exposed. Martin really liked this part.

He patiently watched each woman and their instructor who led them in tribal dances. At times they bent at the waist and swung their heads around, hair flying wildly. The music was mostly drum beats and Martin reached over and took a piece of roll with his fingers, sneaked a quick peek for the soy sauce, dipped and popped it into his mouth. He did use the chopsticks for extra ginger slices but only when there was a break in the dancing. For a half hour this continued and the drum beats and exercises intensified. Sweat dripped off the dancers' bodies. Finally the instructor stopped and turned off the music and clapped for her students. Martin clapped along with her. They clapped back and hugged each other and ran off to shower and change.

Martin had good views of Mandy, Betty Ann and Marci and of course the other women who he didn't know and didn't have time to get to know in the locker room. They disappeared into the windowless shower and Martin poured the last of the sake and put his treat on the table in front of him. In a state of arousal he undressed and stood waiting.

The girls came out of the shower all jiggley and talking and then Marci walked over to the window in her altogether and looked out directly at Martin's window. She was soon joined by Betty Ann and then Mandy. They had their arms around each other's shoulders and began swaying side to side and Martin was mesmerized by their gorgeous bodies, smiling faces and swaying boobs. He was at premium arousal.

They began waving to Martin, blowing him kisses and they bent down and each picked up a piece of cardboard with one word – **HAPPY BIRTHDAY MARTIN**. They held the signs just below their breasts.

Martin, surprised beyond belief, but for some reason not embarrassed by his nakedness, reached up and turned on the overhead light, and waved back. He waved with one hand and then two, arms flying back and forth. Then he toasted them with his sake and they clapped their hands and he popped the sea urchin with raw quail's egg into his mouth and washed it down with the remaining sake, dribbling a little of the quail yoke and sake down to his chin. The girls waved goodbye and left to dress as Martin turned off his light and went back about his business while looking through his binoculars.

The drum music began again, only louder this time. Martin poured soy sauce over his hands, standing and swaying to the drums, and began to pleasure himself and never heard the key in the lock or heard the door opening.

Banzai! Martin yelled at the exact same time the lights came on.

He looked over and saw the dance instructor pointing at him and two policemen standing beside her. Still gripping himself, he slumped satisfied back onto his chair.

Smart
by Michael Webb

I could tell from the growing silence in the house that drunkenness and fatigue were taking over most of the adults as the day slid into evening, so, like it or not, Chandler was my charge until one of them came to. Which was fine. 4.45pm's TV options bored him, so he had happily watched a Spongebob DVD on my laptop, and then some long documentary about trains, while I sat studying his rapt face, wondering what he thinks of this long day full of nothing. At the end, he yawned big and wide, then climbed off me to use the bathroom.

He returns, one finger of his left hand parked in his mouth, which tells me he is getting sleepy. I didn't intend to become the shepherd of lost children, but it is the most graceful way to get away from all of the noise and expectations of family.

He settles down again on the floor between my thighs, the laptop calmly displaying my desktop in front of us both. He leans into me, his head on the muscle below my shoulder, his breath hot on the bare skin above my breastbone.

"Auntie Tay?" he says. I'm not his aunt, but he has been referring to his female relatives as "Aunt" lately. It is simpler not to correct him.

"Yes, baby?"

"Do you know not scary stories?"

"Not scary stories?"

"Yeah," he says, his speech garbled and lisping by the finger he won't remove. "I no like scary ones."

"I don't know a lot of stories, Chandler. Did you bring any storybooks in your backpack? I can read you one of those."

"OK," he says softly. He crawls on all fours to his blue backpack, and extracts a slim volume, then reaches again and pulls out a plastic bag, and then crawls back into place, resting his head against me. I set my laptop aside. He opens the bag, which contains two sad looking animal crackers, what looks like an elephant and a giraffe. They could have been in his backpack for a month. His tiny hand withdraws them.

"Want to share, Auntie Tay?"

"No, thank you, honey," I say. "You can have them both." He stuffs the brown shapes into his mouth.

I begin to read. After a few pages, I feel him growing slack, his weight against me more profound. It's pleasant, the pressure, the gentle heat, the trust that lets him relax. I want to warn him that I'm not trustworthy, that he can't depend on me, that I'm broken and vulnerable and full of need, but he only sinks deeper against me. After the first book is finished, I ease him up onto my bed, intending to get out another book and continue reading.

"Lay down wi' me," he mumbles, and I can do nothing but comply. I lay prone beside him, and he picks his head up and lays it on my shoulder again, above my breast, his breath on my skin again. He puts his hand on my belly, where it rises and falls when I breathe. I feel him relaxing again, almost melting, his breaths coming even and slow. I don't mean to, but I fall asleep as well.

I awaken to the sun casting low, sharp shadows on my floor, Chandler still relaxed and sweaty against my side, and my aunt, her face red and blotched, looming over both of us.

I look up at her, and watch her expertly scoop her son into her arms, where he stirs and then breathes deeply again. "Thank you, Tay," she whispers. "I hope he wasn't any trouble."

"Of course," I say, my own voice thick and soft. "No trouble. We watched a video, and then a story, and then he fell —"

"In the future, hun," she says, cutting me off, "just so you know, we don't sleep with him. He has to learn how to sleep on his own. When you have babies, you'll learn. You're always so good with him, such a smart girl. I'm surprised you didn't know that." She steps to my door.

I feel stunned, and then anger flashes. You know what? I think. How about you not get drunk if you don't like how I watch your kid? How about that? I measure the possible repercussions of speaking out, then think better of it. There are some fights that you never win.

"Goodbye, Tay," she whispers. "Thanks again," and then shuts the door.

Bread without Crusts
by Susan Tepper

Several hours later, I take the loaf of white bread from the cupboard. I decide to make it a little extra special for his dinner. For dinner I will cut off his crusts.

I take the wooden handle knife and quickly slice the crusts off. The bread, without its crusts, looks naked. This makes me shiver. Maybe I should have left the crusts on. I think of them together, naked, doing all the things he used to do with me.

"Fuck this shit," I say.

But I keep staring at the naked white bread. I can't stop staring. It's a lot smaller without its crusts. It looks ragged. Pathetic, actually.

I hear him coming up the basement stairs. We both know our days together are numbered. I figure by the time the loaf is done, we'll be done too.

"What happened to the bread?" he asks.

"I cut off the fucking crusts."

He hitches up his shorts. "Why'd you do that?"

"Aren't you cold in those fucking shorts?"

"Not really." He coughs. "I don't feel much of anything."

Oh! Obviously the way he didn't feel much of anything for me or the marriage.

"Yes, well I can understand that," I say.

"Can you?"

"What do you want on your dinner sandwich?" Again I've got The Baby clutched on my hip.

He moves toward the window over the sink, staring out. "There's a deer," he says.

"You want deer meat on your sandwich?"

He turns around looking confused. "What do you mean?"

"Well, I figured if you want deer meat you can go outside and kill that fucking deer the way you killed me."

"Jesus!" He yanks out a chair and sits down hard. So hard the wooden chair bangs the floor. "I've had enough," he says. "It can't go on like this."

"Oh, really?" He looks weak. It bolsters my spirits. I go to the refrigerator taking out the jar of mayo.

"Is there some ham or roast beef?" he says. "Why do you have to hold her like that?"

"Like what?"

"Like she's not a baby worth holding with both arms." He pauses. "Like you're holding a ham."

"You saying The Baby looks like a ham?"

"Look ... well sort of! Her face is always red and you hold her like a food product."

"Oh, really? Maybe it's because you want a ham that you see a ham in The Baby. Did that ever cross your fucking mind?"

"Do you have any ham in the fridge?"

I can see the hope flicker in his eyes and it only makes me more furious.

"Nope. Only this fucking mayo. Unless you want to cook The Baby."

He jumps out of the chair, screaming, "You bitch!"

Ignoring his tirade, I grab a spoon and ladle mayo onto the white bread in globs.

"You've gone too far!" he's screaming.

Now the baby is really off the rails. "Look what you've done!" I jiggle her on my hip. "There, there, Baby."

"I'm giving her a name. I'm calling her Julia," he says.

"No you're not. I'm her mother."

He finally looks me in the eye. We're in a dead heat. "And I'm her father."

"Maybe. And maybe not." Of course he is the father. But I'll use every weapon in the arsenal. "By the way, you know what they say about people who don't like mayo."

He shakes his head looking weary, beaten. "What do they say?"

"That it's sperm aversion. You or your girlfriend ever heard that one?"

He shrugs.

"Well, I hate mayo. As you know," I say. "I hate it like poison. But I don't have sperm aversion. Remember?" The Baby is yelling at its worst. Julia. It's not a bad name. "Fucking strange, right? So fucking strange." I hand him the plate with his globbed on mayo sandwich. "Enjoy!"

5.10pm
Oakville, Ontario, Canada

Legs Like Stilts
by Cindy Matthews

I push a metal trolley filled with plastic food trays through the corridor of the medical floor. After I managed to get Bob so upset, my boss reassigned me from psych to this floor.

"Last chance," my supervisor, Chad had said. "Get your shit together, man."

I have to work until 7.00pm and this day feels like it just won't end. The medical floor smells of soiled bedding, antiseptic, and minty banana. My throat clenches and I gag. I blame my cranky mood on the pimples that earlier erupted all over my chin.

I pass a large family. They're arguing.

"I swear, Daddy. Visiting hours don't start until later. You didn't even bother to read the sign. You're going to get us all into trouble," says a young woman, her short body draped in a sari.

"Your grandmother expects us to come now and I cannot disappoint her, can I?" says an older man who spits the words out like he's biting them in half. The young woman inherited her father's large nose.

I shoot a glance out a corridor window before leaning against a wall. My legs feel heavy. I notice a peach-coloured vase on the windowsill holds a wilting bouquet of roses that remind me of how fatigued I am. Raindrops ping against the glass. Indigo clouds dance on the roof of the insurance company across the way. I'm not certain but it seems as if it's rained every day this April.

Each supper container on my trolley is labeled with a number and letter corresponding to a patient's bed and room. Easy, I think. Can't screw this up.

In half an hour I've distributed trays to every room except Bed 2 in 807. I'm near the end of shift and the day has been a trying one. Truth is, I've learned a lot and have managed to escape emptying a single bedpan. All I want is to frit away the last couple of minutes playing Candy Crush in the utility closet.

Instead I head to the nursing station to inquire about 807's dinner. My feet squeak to a stop on the floor. This is an opportunity for me to shine, to demonstrate myself as a responsible self-starter. After all, I had a dismal showing early this morning on the children's cancer floor. How was I to know that the letters NPO were Latin for nothing by mouth? To be fair, the hospital did not properly cover that topic in the one-day staff training. My afternoon didn't fare much better with Bob, the crazy fool who set fire to his home.

After I dump the contents of a tray into a trash bin, I scrounge around the other food trolleys for uneaten food. I will redeem myself by finding 807 something to eat. The majority of patients have slurped down the mush the kitchen staff prepared. On one food tray I locate an unopened container of diced peaches, the kind that parents pack for their kids' lunches. On another tray there's a Styrofoam bowl of beef broth. I sniff it. It smells homemade but I know it's most likely from a can. A sliver of cheddar with a toothpick hat has begun to curl. I push a sleeve of unsalted crackers into my pocket.

I carry the tray into 807. The satin edge of a turquoise blanket is folded under a woman's breasts. Her eyes are closed but I know she's not asleep because she's humming. Her shoulders and back of her head lean against the headboard. A pillow has slid under her mid-back so her stomach sticks out and the position looks uncomfortable. She hums again, a little louder, like she wants to find the correct pitch. It sounds like some Broadway hit – maybe *Cats*. She opens her eyes. They are bloodshot and moist.

"Hey, aren't you the kid from this morning?"

I square my shoulders, bristling at her use of the word *kid*.

It's the woman with the cigarette. From the sidewalk this morning. I still recognize her from somewhere else but damned if I can remember where or what. All I know is she's the one with legs like stilts. She's wearing a nightgown from home, not the dull blue, institutional ones that look a tad drabber than the uniforms we orderlies wear. Hers is the kind grown-up kids buy their moms. It's a light green thing with muted yellow flowers. There's a dash of lace on the collar.

"Yes, we met earlier. Outside, I believe," I say. She'd caught me ogling her. She points at the tray in my hands.

"Food – for me? Finally. Because I'm closer than I've ever been to starving." Her eyes close for a moment before she says, "No one has been around to feed me all day. What's the matter with this place?"

Her eyes lock on me like she'd sooner gnaw the green plastic food tray in my hands than wait another second for the real thing.

I gulp. I've been here before. There's an IV tube taped to the back of her hand and another thin hose snaking up her nostrils. The room doesn't have a blue water jug like all the

181

others. I glance at the door. No evidence of tape residue. Behind the door. Nada. No pink sign. Worried for nothing.

I look back at the patient. Her eyes are bugging from her face. She rips the plastic tube from her nose, then grips my arm, and screams, "Give me that goddamned tray!"

"Code blue response team. Report to 815. Code blue response team."

"Ma'am, let me go check on that announcement," I say. I pry her fingers from my wrist. Pinch marks from her nails bloom along my skin.

Cardiac arrest. I feel energized by the urgency of the hospital announcement and jog toward the nursing station in search of help. No one is there. I hear a second all-call. I turn around and race back to 807, my feet beating fast against the floor.

I stand by the door of the room, place my thumbs in the waistband of my scrubs, and chew my bottom lip. The green tray is upside down on the floor beside the bed. The patient has tipped her IV pole over. Fluid puddles beside the nightstand. Miss Stilt Legs is curled up on the floor. Her tongue is licking the base of the cup of peaches. She looks up at me and smiles funny, syrup glistening from her chin.

Blood and Soil
by Desmond Fox

I slip out of the hole into the uneasy orange city night, but only as far as my nose. The same slaughter of smells hangs heavy over the sun-beaten grass; pink meat fat, burnt flesh, petrol fumes, beer urine: barbeque season in the park. If you are smart, if you want to live, then you must wait. Then you must learn to live with your own thoughts, and be played by your own memories, and doubt if the memories are your own.

Do you know how long the smell of blood stays in the earth? That is what we call 'history'. There are rich fields of it here, mounds and streams and rivers of it.

That was a time of great movement, when the world was turned upside down. People moved out of their crumbled buildings and hid in the woods. Badgers were pushed out of the parks and moved into the collapsed cellars on Hermannstraße. A man lived in a hole under a tree, and he lived by foraging. His house was taken by the badger. There were bats under the half-a-roof, songbirds in the upper bedroom, a fox in the empty larder.

The zoo was hit. The hippo boiled in his tank. The elephant was cut by stray metal, and the neighbours kept cutting until she was bone. And the next in line took the bone.

The trees were burned, blasted, cut for firewood. The owls and bats moved onto what was left of the people's houses. The people moved into what was left of their basements.

And while the people starved and tried to grow potatoes in the park the owls fattened on rats, the birds fattened on flies, and the rats and flies found plenty to eat. What the rats got fat on. That was when the rats and flies swarming had their own noise.

Will the taste ever leave? That's what happens when you've had every meat the city has to offer.

6.00pm
Belmont, Massachusetts, USA

Dinner
by Gloria Garfunkel

I dread what will show up on my plate tonight. Something so gross I can't look at it. Then my husband and two teen-aged sons appear with a bunch of white paper and plastic bags of real food. Croissants, scones and several dishes of my favorite Chinese food. My sweet family brought me all the foods I love. Little vegetable dumplings, vegetarian moo-shi, garlic watercress, and spicy string beans.

Mathew, my older son, puts my tray of disgusting hospital dinner on a back table.

"What is that food?" he asks.

"I have no idea," I say.

I am in heaven. I eat a whole plate of Chinese food and save the pastries for breakfast.

Then they bring out the chocolate cupcakes.

"Happy birthday, Mom!"

"It's my birthday?" I say. "I forgot."

I start to cry.

"We love you, Mom," both my children say.

"Don't try to talk," says Mathew, my older son.

"Don't cry," says Christopher, my younger one.

"You'll be OK soon," says my husband, though I know this is not true.

"Why don't they just order take-out for the patients?" says Christopher. He is very practical. "I bet it would be even cheaper per patient than cooking this crap themselves."

"And they'd be happier and get well faster," says Mathew.

The nurses all comment on the great smell of the Chinese food in my room long after the leftovers have been dumped in their trashcan. I think they are jealous.

A Cold Dinner
by Kyle Hemmings

The sky is star-studded and the night is breezy. Kit is in Czarina's kitchen making a *kletsky*, which is a chicken broth with potato dumplings. It was one of the first dishes that Czarina ever showed her how to make. Kit thinks that this will be good for Czarina's "cold", because that's what Czarina has been complaining of, off and on. Czarina is resting in the bedroom, dozing in and out of sleep.

"Czarina!" calls out Kit.

No reply.

"Mama," she yells.

She hears a faint voice, as if from somewhere far.

"Yes," Czarina says, "I'm coming."

Kit knows that it will take her time to dress.

"Do you need help?"

"No."

"You really must see a doctor. If I have to drag you."

What she really wants to tell Czarina is that she will stop hustling and get a job at a local diner that her "friend" suggested. Dasha is good friends with one of the managers.

In the kitchen, Kit cooks the potatoes in salted water then mashes them with butter. She then adds eggs, pepper, and basil and some flour. She mixes the ingredients into the potato, sometimes adding more flour, until it is firm. She then divides the mixture into small dumplings.

"Mama, are you alright?"

"Yes."

Czarina's voice is still soft and faraway.

Kit adds chicken pieces, dumplings, veggies, and bouquet garni to the pot. She brings the ingredients to a boil. Then she adds the peppercorns and lets the soup simmer. Occasionally she skims the water with a large spoon. Then, she strains the soup through a cheesecloth, just the way Czarina had showed her, and into a large bowl. She seasons with salt. She is not sure if she did everything in the correct order but it tastes good to her.

"It's ready," calls out Kit. "Mama! Come."

The woman must have fallen asleep again, she thinks. Kit pours some of the soup into a small bowl and brings it to Czarina.

In the bedroom, Czarina is half-dressed and is lying on the bed. Her limbs are flaccid; her face is ashen. There is no rise and fall of her chest.

The bowl of soup crashes to the floor, splashing on Kit's new pumps, spreading under the bed.

Kit feels for a pulse. Nothing. She whips out a cell phone from her pocket and dials 911. In a frenzied voice, she gives the operator all the necessary information, although she must repeat certain things, like the address.

Kit jumps to the bed, gives mouth to mouth resuscitation, feels Czarina's ribs crack below her palms.

Weight Watching
by Gloria Garfunkel

At home, I usually have no appetite until dinner and just starve all day except for lots of coffee, tea, orange juice and water. Here I have no appetite at all. The Chinese food and cup cakes buoyed my mood and revived my appetite. I feel a little bit normal again.

The doctors show up on their daily rounds and ask me about my issues with food. I say I am overweight from blowing up from the poisoning though I wasn't sure what my weight was at this time.

"I need to diet, but I eat … um … vegan foods, like salads. But I'm so fat now I look … um … pregnant." They glance at each other like I am psychotic.

I have discovered that the less I eat, the flatter my stomach gets, and the less I want to eat. I never count calories like obsessive anorexics. I don't purge like bulimics. I don't take diet pills. I don't over-exercise. In fact, I don't exercise at all except for picking up dust bunnies in our house because we have lots of rugs and I never vacuum. I am definitely not eating-disordered.

My metabolism is screwed up from the poisoning. I gained a pound a day for a month.

So what is a normal weight for someone who is my height, which a nurse measures at 5'2", a number I seem to remember. The nurse says 104 to 131 pounds. I think she weighs me at 140 but I'm not sure if that comes before or after 104. I think I want to be 100, a round easy number to remember, but I am also not sure if that falls in or out of the spectrum.

Dinner and Call It a Night
by Walter Giersbach

The city looked like an Edward Hopper painting, rain sheeting on Sixth Avenue, a miasma of fog swirling up from the Con Edison steam tunnels under the street. Cars swooshed south toward the maw of the Lincoln Tunnel and an escape to Jersey. Manhattan was an impressionist landscape and death seemed to say, *C'mon, you mortals, you'll love it where you're going!*

With a perfectly straight face, Mike had told the chick at the maître d's lectern, "A table for one, unless Mayor DeBlasio stops by and asks for me."

Now he was dry under the awning of the West Village sidewalk cafe. And his glass of Brooklyn Beer, the last of its artisanal winter ale, was dry. Dry was good. Not so good was the fact that his brain also was dry of ideas. He had the characters of his novel clear, down to their toenails, hooves and claws; but they were inanimate, lifeless as clockwork toys that had come unwound. Lucy and the other characters were waiting in the wings, anticipating a story line that would bring them to life on the stage. Inspiration had taken off, leaving him bereft of any shred of creativity. Damn that woman! Damn her for distracting him with her irritating dramas.

He had to re-enter his characters' lives. What would Lucy Dingo order at a sidewalk cafe? An angelic potion that frothed over the lip of the glass? He sipped his ale and scanned his phone for messages. Nothing there. No texts, no e-mails, no calls. *Nada, nichts, rien.* Then, looking up in shock, he saw Calliope shambling along Fourth Street with her head down. She was the Queen of Mean, but she was a living, breathing person to relieve his loneliness.

"Calliope Katsanakis," he called, "as I live and breathe. You're still alive."

"You," she said tonelessly.

"Buy you dinner?" he asked with false brightness. "We'll go Dutch treat because we forgive each other. I'll order the appetizers, you choose the entree, then I'll select a tasty *amuse bouche*, and you get dessert. A simple meal."

She walked over to the railing and stood with her arms wrapped around her waist. "You confuse me, Mike. Really, I've never known anyone like you. You turn my brain into some sort of smoothie coming out of my ears like my head was a blender."

"C'mon in out of the rain. On your way, tell the lady at the lectern you're Mayor Bill DeBlasio's sister. He's been delayed."

Calliope yanked the black watch cap from her hair. She shrugged off the hip-length leather jacket and memories of the rain and plumped down in the chair he had pulled out for her. Mascara-rimmed eyes completed the picture of a Village biker chick.

"Love your outfit. Sort of Lauren Bacall channeling Marlon Brando."

"Just get me a drink. Johnny Walker Black, one cube of ice, please. It's been a bitch of a day."

"Peace treaty, okay? *Pax.* Later we can smoke a peace pipe." He reached out and touched her cold hand, letting it go as the waitress approached to take their order.

"Whatever."

"What do you think the odds are, running into each other in New York three times in one day?" He punched the air dramatically, hoping to see some lights go on inside her face. "This must really screw up the cosmic odds. I bet Jesus and Buddha and Mohammed are scratching their heads over this one."

"Yeah, sure."

"You don't believe in karma? Serendipity? Happenstance?"

"Here comes my drink, and I bet you need a refill," she said. "I noticed that when your mouth is full you don't talk as much."

"Kelly," he said, using her nickname for the first time, "earlier today, at lunch, you called me an honorable man." He chose his words as carefully as if he'd bitten into a forkful of steamed trout, watchful that there were no bones to choke him to death. "But you said it, like, wistfully. Like wishful thinking. Like you weren't sure." The words slipped out of his mouth and surprised him in their candor. Was his subconscious taking leave of his protective custody without even a goodbye note?

There was a long pause, he watching her while she watched traffic. "Because I'm not an honorable woman."

"I know. You're a call girl. Whores don't really have a heart of gold. That's just a cliché."

"That wouldn't make me dishonorable. Just stupid or money-hungry or venal." She seemed to shrink, her shoulders folding inward. "No, I lied. I'm just a girl who was let go from her job in the magazine business. I was an editorial assistant, but now I'm not. I'm broke. But it's no lie that I owe $26,000 in student loans." She ran her finger around the top of her glass. "When you found me, I was a little bit drunk and a lot of depressed, just wondering what life was worth."

"And the mob's going to find you because you know about ..."

"No, I lied about that too. To get some sympathy. To make you want to feel sorry for me."

"Kelly," he said, "I don't feel *sorry*. I thought about you today. How you face up to a hostile world. I feel respect because you show *chutzpah, cojones, sangfroid*."

"Jesus, you can talk meaninglessly in three languages!" She snorted. A smile teased the corner of her mouth.

"I'm the one who needs the understanding. It was my mom who died this week. Her loft I'm living in. She wasn't a warm and loving mother, but she was the only family I had left except for a brother imitating a missing person. Taking care of her gave me some purpose because my books aren't selling. And writing and drawing are the only talents I have."

This time she lifted the glass, examined the golden whiskey, swirled it and sipped. "New York is a place for lonely people, like some eddy in a stream where all the floating stuff collects and goes around in a circle."

"Well, maybe the floating objects can meet up and get to know each other."

"What," she asked, "what if your next story was about a whole young generation that's been flimflammed by the promise of unachievable hopes, shattered by fabricated wars that turned soldiers into psychotic monsters, suffered under political cynicism unknown since that Roman guy Caligula? And now every moment of their lives is monitored by the same engines of progress that promised improvements."

"A story torn from the headlines!"

She hunched forward. "But there's this sympathetic super-woman able to call up miracles and there's a righteous heroic writer who's lost his way in the dark underbelly of the city's economic collapse, our dystopian future and the crushed spirits of the people. Together, they team up and save the forlorn and deserving people."

A cartoonish light bulb went off over his head. "She's looking for an opportunity to prove her hyper-normal talents ..."

"... And he's seeking redemption from his grief and feeling betrayed by a great loss," she finished.

"I think it might work. I can visualize the story line."

"You think I'm ballsy, so I'm going to say something. Ready? Creative pairing." She leaned back in triumph.

"Like those arty carved vegetables sushi chefs do, with their paring ..."

"No, jerk. Pairing, like Lennon and McCartney, Romeo and Juliet, Laurel and Hardy." She hunched forward and grabbed Mike's wrists. "I think and you draw. Being an editorial assistant was just getting my foot in the door to ..."

"You know, I think my publisher, Saltzman, needs someone to get him organized. He's looking for an assistant. Someone articulate and organized, and with keyboard skills. And it doesn't hurt to be good-looking."

"You think we could carry this off, this creative togetherness thing? I mean, unless it got too heavy. Then we'd have to go our separate ways or kill each other."

Mike couldn't remember the last time a woman had looked at him intently, shooting rays of concentration at his brain. Sincerity was such a rare commodity in New York.

"I'll choose the appetizers," he said decisively. "You look at the menu and make up our mind what we're going to have for the main course."

She laughed. "Then a little something to tickle our palate, whatever it was you called it."

"*Amuse bouche.* French for a little tidbit before the courses."

195

"You're speaking of an intercourse? That sounds *very* interesting."

Mike reached over to enfold Kelly's hand. "Did you know Lucy Dingo is a New Yorker? In its own way, this tough city is an island for heroes like her. Like us. Some of them are defeated and fall to the curbside. Others are made of stronger stuff, and it helps if they've wandered these streets. The magic is when two heroes find each other among eight million people."

She nodded. "Peter Pan said it best. All it takes is faith and trust, and a little bit of pixie dust."

The New Czarina
by Kyle Hemmings

The rooms feel cold and she doesn't wish to be alone. Kit will be sleeping with Czarina's ghost for a long time, perhaps forever.

Dasha arrives, takes off her jacket and hugs Kit, kisses her on the forehead.

"You're shaking," Dasha whispers in her ear.

Kit takes Dasha by the hand into the kitchen.

"You see that pot?" she says pointing to it. "Well, it was for me and Mama. But she can't be here. So you are my new Czarina. And there is still plenty for the both of us."

Dasha smiles and nods gently.

The two girls face each other at the table. And as hard as it is to eat without thinking of what happened, Kit works up a smile at Dasha.

"It is good?" asks Kit.

"It is good," says Dasha.

"Will you live with me?" asks Kit.

Food for Thought
by Tom Fegan

The dread of April 24th was over. Night draped the city as I sat at the Stockyards Café studying the menu. Earle Bowles had happily informed me that Ben Tomlinson had accepted a plea bargain of 30 years to run concurrently with his current sentence of 50. He confessed to murdering Gerry Day. Bowles laughed and told me after speaking with the suspect's lawyer, he called his father as well. Joseph Tomlinson was a retired 30-year veteran of the Fort Worth Police and had a distinguished record. It was his father who convinced Ben to do what was right.

"His attorney told me that boy hung his head and said 'yes sir' to his old man," Bowles had chuckled, "Your efforts were okay too, Jonson. The evidence helped me work this deal. Take care." The conversation was over my cell phone as I'd walked back to the station. Bowles would take the bows for being a judicious public servant and elected official. I could clear the case from my desk. I thought of the Day family. I had informed them of the outcome and they promised to be at the parole hearings and protest Tomlinson ever being released.

My stomach growled as I scanned the entrees. The thought of a succulent prime rib steak, baked potato with sour cream and chives, salad and a dessert of double chocolate layered cake enticed my taste buds. I ordered the

Cobb Salad with hot tea and side order of garlic bread. The latter was a little cheat on my diet, but not a big one. The doctor expected some of that; the cholesterol medicine had to work on something to keep me healthy.

I ordered and gave the young lady my menu. Her shapely figure melted into her tight uniform. I guessed a college student working part time. When my order arrived and I began eating I realized how easy it is to do what is right, whether ordering healthy food or living an orderly life. I saw it every day. The wrong choice always leads to a destructive path. The right choice may be a difficult way, but the benefits will reap. It takes honest hard work.

I tore a piece of garlic bread and munched on it and returned to the salad. When the meal was finished the day would be over. I could rest easy on a full stomach and clear conscience.

Howard and Maggie
by Jonathan Levy

It was nine o'clock, and the stars shone brightly over Comfort, Texas. Howard Fletcher sat in a lawn chair in the backyard of his small brick home, holding a glass of milk. Next to him sat another lawn chair, empty, though in it, Howard saw his wife, Maggie.

"Well, hello, dear. Did you enjoy your birthday today?"

It was a lovely birthday.

Howard raised his glass and took a sip. "And a nice dinner, too. Doesn't Al make the best caesar salad?"

Yes, dear.

"I'm happy for Al and Cara. They're an adorable couple." He sipped again then wiped the milk mustache off his lip. "Will you be spending the night?"

I have to go, Howard.

Howard nodded slowly. "Where do you go?"

It's not time for you to know.

"Take me with you. I miss you, Maggie. All the time."

Maggie stood, walked to Howard's side, and knelt. She clasped her hand in his empty one. A gust of wind swept up Howard's arm then whispered down his back. His shoulders shook as he shivered.

You really want to?

"Please." Howard placed the glass of milk on the ground, sat back up, and breathed in, ready.

Maggie placed her free hand over Howard's chest. His eyes closed, then his heart slowed until it stopped.

Mothra
by Gloria Garfunkel

I start to remember what it was like at home just before I was hospitalized. A sudden infestation of grain moths drove me crazy. It was bad enough that stationary objects seemed to be moving, but these tiny vermin were flitting all over the house and were impossible to catch. I remember Googling grain moths and it said to empty the source, throw everything out, and vacuum to eliminate the larvae. My husband started to empty a top shelf in the kitchen, the source of the infestation, where we kept all our flour, nuts, oatmeal and raisins, things that grain moths love to eat. They even wormed their way through plastic bags, weaving little webs. We knew we would have to vacuum it out, but not that day. That day I spent in the emergency room and was hospitalized that night, so meanwhile the grain moths were left to our two vigilant cats, jumping up to catch and eat them for entertainment.

"Did you kill all the grain moths yet?" I ask my husband.

"That's great that you remember them," he says. "You're making progress."

But he doesn't answer my question.

How could I not remember them? I had been obsessed. I had started researching Mothra, the good monster who fought the evil but stupid Godzilla. She captivated my imagination, but I still can't keep straight all the stages she went through, including egg, larva, chrysalis, pupa and full moth. I just know that my healing will have to go through stages, too, and right now I am a sedentary egg, my mind flitting like a chamber of moths. I do remember my cats on constant moth patrol, Mothra's little fairy twins. Yes, I remember the moths.

And this I remember as well, without writing it on the wall: my children and husband will love me forever, even if I lose all my words.

Authors

Paul Beckman

has been published widely, in print, online and via audio and video. In 2014 he had four stories in anthologies and so far in 2015 he has fourteen stories due out including in Pure Slush, Pank and Apocrypha & Abstractions. His new collection of Flash Fiction, *Peek* is available now, and you can find his website here: http://paulbeckmanstories.com.

Claudia Bierschenk

lives in Berlin, Germany. In the last eleven months she has produced 300 litres of milk.

Tom Fegan

is a native Texan and lifelong Fort Worth resident. He spent several years in the steel industry after college. Tom is contentedly divorced and works in private security which allows him freedom to read and write.

Lyn Fowler

lives in Perth, Western Australia with her husband. She has two wonderful adult daughters. She is a member of the Fellowship of Australian Writers Western Australia. She participates in a writers group, Booklength Project Group, that meets once a month for support and friendship. She has attended several writing workshops and has written family and travel memoir. Currently she is working on a novel, inspired by her travels. Her passion for Mediterranean food and culture is never far from her writing.

Desmond Fox

1968: Milk, sugar & mashed bananas.
1969: White bread with meat paste.
1970: Biscuits (Lincoln, Bourbons, Custard Creams).
1971: Sausages. Baked beans. Cheese.
1972 – 1986: Boiled-potatoes, -peas, -carrots, -cabbage,
    meat.
1973: Chocolate, Smarties, Choc Ice.
1976: Frozen-fish fingers, -potato waffles, -savoury
    pancakes.
1987: Garlic, pasta, curry.
1991: Tuna melt on toast.
1996: Burger with a pickle.
1997: Chicken with peanut sauce.
1998: Thai curry with coconut sauce.

Gloria Garfunkel

is a psychologist and writer with a Ph.D. from Harvard University in Psychology and Social Relations. A former psychotherapist, she has published many stories in literary journals and anthologies.

Walter Giersbach

bounces between writing genres, from mystery to humor, speculative fiction to romance. His work has appeared in print and online in over a score of publications. Two volumes of short stories, *Cruising the Green of Second Avenue*, are available at Barnes & Noble, Amazon and other online booksellers. He's also bounced from Fortune 500 firms to university posts, and from homes in eight states and to a couple of Asian countries. He now writes and moderates a writing group in New Jersey.

Kyle Hemmings

lives and works in New Jersey. He has been published in Your Impossible Voice, Night Train, Toad, Matchbox and elsewhere. His latest ebook is *Father Dunne's School for Wayward Boys* at amazon.com, and you can find his blog at http://upatberggasse19.blogspot.com/.

Gill Hoffs

lives in Warrington, England, with her family, Coraline Cat and never quite enough cake. A non-fiction piece included in her first book *Wild: a collection* (Pure Slush Books, 2012) led to her writing the history book *The Sinking of RMS Tayleur: The Lost Story of the 'Victorian Titanic'* (Pen & Sword, 2014). Questions answered and chocolate accepted via gillhoffs@hotmail.co.uk and @GillHoffs on twitter.

Jonathan Levy

currently lives in Raleigh, NC, with his wife and two dogs. He began writing fiction in late 2013, and so far the staff and readers of Boston Literary Magazine, Pure Slush, Tell Us a Story, Paper Tape, r.kv.r.y quarterly, and Cafe Irreal have made him feel so grateful and lucky.

Cindy Matthews

has worked as a chambermaid, potato peeler, data entry operator, teacher, and vice-principal of special education programs. She writes, paints, and instructs online courses from her studio office in rural Ontario, Canada. Her fiction and non-fiction have appeared in magazines / online in Canada, USA, Australia, and the UK. Find her work at http://cindymatthews.ca.

AR Neal

got bit by the writing bug in the 1970s and despite a career in education has never been cured of her penchant for speculative fiction. Her most recent book, *After*, is available on Amazon.com, and you can find more of her work at http://starvingactivist.com.

Mandy Nicol

grew up in Melbourne, Australia and made a tree change to country Victoria in the mid-nineties – the decade, not her age. She has various animals including a flockette of pet sheep that are thankful for her vegaquarian habits. She writes short stories and loves flash fiction.

Matt Potter

is an Australian-born writer who keeps a part of his psyche in Berlin. Matt has been published in various places online, and he is, rather amazingly, also the founding editor of *Pure Slush*, and thus the publisher of this book! You can find more of his work at http://mattcpotter.webs.com/.

Andrew Stancek

grew up in Bratislava and saw tanks rolling through its streets. On occasion he has claimed direct descent from Janosik, the Slovak Robin Hood. He writes, dreams and entertains Muses in Ontario. His work has appeared in Tin House online, Every Day Fiction, fwriction, Necessary Fiction, Prime Number Magazine, Camroc Press Review and Blue Five Notebook. He's been a winner in the Flash Fiction Chronicles and Gemini Fiction Magazine contests and been nominated for a Pushcart Prize.

Susan Tepper

is the author of four published books of fiction and a chapbook of poetry. Her current title *The Merrill Diaries* (Pure Slush Books, 2013) is a Novel in Stories. Tepper is Second Place Winner in story/South Million Writers Award for 2014, the recipient of nine Pushcart Nominations, and a Pulitzer nomination for her novel *What May Have Been* (co-written with Gary Percesepe). She writes a monthly column called *Let's Talk* at Black Heart Magazine, hosts FIZZ a reading series at KGB Bar in NYC, and moderates the Indie Press Panel each June at Hunter College Writers Conference. Find more about Susan at her website here: http://www.susantepper.com.

Michael Webb

has been reading and writing since approximately the time of the cooling of the Earth's crust. His work has been seen at Metazen, The Broken Plate, and in *The Lost Children Charity Anthology*, as well as on his own website, which you can find at http://michaelwebb.us.

Allan J. Wills

lives in a small town among the forests of Western Australia with his Japanese wife and young son. His day job is in the field of forest entomology, and he has co-authored a body of published scientific writing on forest entomology. Flash fiction provides a new challenge for him, with its demand for drawing complete engagement of the reader within the constraint of concision.

Other books from Pure Slush

Jan Feb March 2014
ISBN: 978-1-925101-33-1

April May June 2014
ISBN: 978-1-925101-46-1

July Aug Sept 2014
ISBN: 978-1-925101-47-8

Oct Nov Dec 2014
ISBN: 978-1-925101-48-5

Many Fish to Fry
ISBN: 978-1-925101-59-1

The Vixen Scream
ISBN: 978-1-925101-11-9

www.ingramcontent.com/pod-product-compliance
Lightning Source LLC
Chambersburg PA
CBHW050528260626
47157CB00004B/1520